Look out for **BAD HEIST** by Ernest McQueen later in 2021. The long-awaited second book featuring Ted Bird and Betty Abbett from Mad Dog Crime is available for pre-order right now at

**www.maddogbooks.uk**

You can also sign up for our free email newsletter. Subscribers get free gifts, discounts and first news of our latest titles.

## THE GUN SLIPPED

When private investigators Ted Bird and Betty Abbett are hired by a local shipping tycoon to investigate a smuggling racket, they quickly find themselves in the frame for murder.

As Ted struggles to unravel the truth, another man disappears at sea. The net is closing in. Could their client be lying to them? Is anyone they meet being straight? This is a high stakes story of greed, piracy, murder and international intrigue.

We're excited to bring you a new gumshoe detective, Edward Bird. Known to his enemies as Ted Bod, he works with his boss, Betty Abbett, to clean up the port city of 1950s Kingstown. Ted is a totally new British crime hero for the modern reader.

## About the Author

Ernest McQueen is a new British gumshoe noir writer in the American hardboiled tradition. Inspired by the greats, such as Raymond Chandler, Dashiell Hammett, Robert B. Parker, Ross Macdonald and James Crumley, McQueen writes about 1950s Britain in a way that appeals directly to the 2020s crowd. *The Gun Slipped* is his first novel, and he is working on the second book in the series, *Bad Heist*.

**Other Books by WTD Books / Mad Dog Crime**

*by Paul Charles*
From Beyond Belief / The Playground
Kicking Tin

*by P. C. DETTMANN*
Paul Locksley
Nikoo Hayek
Ernest Zevon
Jorja Pearson

*by Ernest McQueen*
The Gun Slipped
Bad Heist

Mad Dog Crime presents

# THE GUN SLIPPED

by Ernest McQueen

*Enjoy!*
*Ern McQueen*

MDC-002

*For Rebecca and Isis,*

# CHAPTER ONE

It all happened down at the docks that night. I didn't expect a gun. I don't think anybody did. But to understand what happened at the docks, there's a bunch of other things you need to understand first. Then you can understand my present situation. Which isn't great, and I've seen some things.

The week had started normally enough, on a Monday, as all right-thinking people agree that it does. I waltzed into the office, full of news about the weekend, expecting a slow crawl out of the grey fog. When it's foggy here, you can hear the horns on the ships. It is a low rumble, like an earthquake, and they have horns to warn each other in the river. Sometimes they crash, but not often.

In the office I found Miss Iris M. Cool, always the first one in. I'm usually second. Betty, that's our boss and the owner of the agency, is always last in. As she pays our wages, it is her prerogative. Miss Cool was hammering away at her typewriter, a cigarette dancing between her red lips until you thought the ash would fall but it never did. While she flings the roller back, what's that called? The carriage. She flings it across with one hand while using the other hand to tap the ash into the ashtray in a synchronised moment. In this way, she has told me before, she can maintain one hundred words per minute without easing off, and still make it through twenty smokes a day. She is multi-talented, that girl.

"Morning, Miss Cool," I said, as cheerfully as I could manage. Never wasting air on talk, she gave me a friendly wink and carried on bashing. It was too early for the post, so I hung my hat and coat on the stand and wandered into my office.

We have an office each, Betty and me. With our names on the frosted glass in gold leaf. She paid for that last year, after one of our cases actually went well and we made more money than expenses. It's a hard game in this town. The docks are always bringing new folk in to keep track of, from all over the world, and as a result crime is higher than the mayor would like it. It's good for us when the clients don't skip town before paying our fees, of course, but it's hard.

I was telling you about the docks and the gun. But this is before then, this is the Monday morning it all started. Unusually, a client turned up early for a morning conference, so that Betty was not in. Normally I would let Miss Cool deal with the interloper, but something told me that she was behind on those letters and that Betty, that's Betty Abbett, the one with her name against our license to practice, that Betty was expecting the letters ready by last Friday night. For these reasons, I found myself walking out to open the door to the client, making him coffee - black, heavy on the sugar - and making small talk. He seemed put out that I wasn't Miss Cool, and you're not to blame him for that.

"It's Partridge," said our client. "Donald Partridge." I hadn't been appraised of his status within our client acquisition process but he acted like I should know the name. I didn't.

"Good morning, sir," I said vaguely. "Are you looking for Betty? Mrs Abbett?"

The man nodded as I handed him the steaming mug. I realised then that it should have been a cup and saucer from the client cupboard.

"Who are you?" asked Partridge.

"I'm one of Betty's operatives, Edward Bird. People always call me Ted."

"Good morning, Ted. When will Betty be here?"

"Any minute. Are you in a hurry? I can try to raise her on the phone, perhaps?"

The man pulled a gold pocket watch from somewhere and shook his head. "I'm eight, nine minutes early. I'll wait."

He plonked himself in the chair and sipped away, so I went back to my office and began tidying up, as I do every Monday. I prefer to do it that way so that I don't have to look for a job while I'm waking up on Mondays. Looking busy when Betty arrived was always a good angle.

I got another wink off Miss Cool for depositing a coffee beside her typewriter. I know little about her other than that she watches *The Grove Family* on television. She can type, smoke and sip at the same time, and that's why she does the typing.

I closed the door on my office and started screwing up paper for the waste basket. I screwed up each sheet I didn't need and threw the balls one at a time into the basket. More than half hit the target. It was in this steady state that the whirlwind that is Betty Abbett blew into the building five minutes later.

"Edward!"

That didn't sound good. I gingerly opened the door, although I could see a wide grey outline on the other side of the glass.

"Edward! With me, please." She lowered her voice after I'd opened the door. I went with her into the adjoining office. It hadn't been tidied in the whole year we had worked together. There were cobwebs in some of the stacks of paperwork, invoices and envelopes. No cheques, of course. They were all carefully cared for and deposited within minutes of arrival.

"Sit down, Ted. I need a quick one about Partridge out there. Why the hell is he early on a Monday?"

Betty watched me sit, but remained on her feet. She was a pacer. There was a groove in her carpet, winding between the objects and piles of paper down there. It was like the Hellfire Pass.

"You know Partridge?" she asked.

I didn't know Partridge.

"I thought not. He's high up in one of the shipping larks over by the docks."

And that was how we came to be at the docks that night.

"Is it his wife?" I asked. It was a safe bet.

"No, smart arse, it's not." Betty didn't like that we only handled divorces, but they made up a fair bulk of her business, our business. "No, friend, this is corporate espionage from the top shelf."

If Betty got going with French words like espionage it was to be taken as a warning. "I want you on this one," she continued, "and I want you to show Partridge in here as soon as you've tidied up the papers. I want you to keep schtum until he's told us the full story, and then do that thing where you ask lots of incisive questions, yes?"

Betty was holding Miss Cool's coffee. She proceeded to demolish it in two gulps. "I will show Mr. Partridge in shortly."

And I found myself tidying the great Betty's office at high knots. I blew some dust, scooped, dumped and finished by pinging open the roller blind with a flourish. She had the only outside window in the place, but with a fog like this it didn't make much difference. Partridge was into the room as I turned around.

"Take a seat, Mr. Partridge. I'm going to be working on your case, so I'll take some notes while Betty talks you through the particulars."

"Just so," he said, and plonked himself in the chair I had been warming a few moments before. Most people are instinctively repelled by a chair that has been warmed by another man's backside. Partridge didn't flinch.

"Right, Mr. Partridge. In your own time, sir." Betty was all smiles.

Partridge cleared his throat. "It sounds simple when you say it. Someone's on the chisel in my organisation."

"The shipping company, Mr Partridge?"

He nodded. "One of my staff is siphoning off some of the stuff we ship, mainly lumber, wood. It's stealing, but covered up on the inside very cleverly. They're not just smuggling it, but covering their tracks too."

"An inside job should be quite easy to unravel, Mr Partridge," I said. "Do you have anyone in mind?"

"I do."

"So why come to us?" asked Betty. It was the obvious question, one I thought she would have asked at their first meeting. The glance she gave me suggested she already knew the answer.

"I'm not confident of my suspicions," he replied quickly. "It could be one of three or four, or more likely several of them colluding. If I start digging around, rumours will get around and they'll either stop or get nasty."

"Wouldn't be such a bad thing if they stopped, I would think." A silence arrived. I wasn't going to be the one to break it. "It's not enough for it to just stop," he said carefully. "I want them caught so they can be... disciplined."

Betty would have sensed my thoughts at this point. We first met in the police more than twenty years ago.

"We will be pleased to act for you, Mr Partridge. And as soon as we can prove who is involved we will present the information to the relevant..."

"It will be enough to just give me their names. If you're convinced of yourselves that's good enough for me."

"How did you hear of us, sir?" I asked.

"I put the word out and more than one person suggested Mrs Abbett here. Your reputation is very high."

Betty smiled despite herself. "Whoever sent you this way has high standards, Mr Partridge. I'll let Miss Cool outside talk you through the terms but it's very simple. You don't want to work on a day rate?"

"What are the alternatives?"

"On a case like this, where we have a list of suspects and a narrow field, we can act for a fixed price. You pay up front and you know how much you're paying out. We don't stop until we're finished, however long it takes."

"And how long will that be?"

"No more than a week," I said flatly. It had to be a colleague. "Write down the names here with their job title or whatever information you can give us including addresses and any telephone numbers, and I'll get started."

"The other advantage of a fixed fee," Betty continued, "is less paperwork for you, and for us too if I'm honest. It's simple and clear and we can guarantee a result in such a case, of course. I stake my reputation on it."

"Sounds good to me, Mrs Abbett. He took out his chequebook. How much?"

"A thousand for a cheque or nine hundred in cash," she said quickly. He carried on writing.

"Eight hundred for cash," she said, and he put the cheques away. He opened his wallet and counted out the money. There was plenty left, I could see, and he sure as hell wanted me to notice.

"I'm on the case right now," I said. "Once I get the names and particulars of the suspects, I'll hit the track."

This part of the job is the part I love the most. In fact, it's the only part I enjoy. You have a list of leads, money in the bank, or in Betty's bank anyway, and every piece of information is new. It's the part I find easy, just chatting to people, even if they don't particularly want to chat to me. That's fun. It beats waving guns around.

So what is going on here? A part of me always takes the story at face value, and that's the best place to start. But the whole time, you have to keep in mind that the story is probably horse crap.

I have in my hand a list of five names, all men. All on the payroll at Partridge's ship company. It's not called Partridge's for obvious reasons. It's called the Lord Line, whatever that refers to. The word "line" often appears in shipping operations because it means a line of ships or boats, literally. The proper steam shipping lines only started in England around a hundred years ago. Of course, we had sailing ships before that, but the modern idea of a shipping line still feels new to most people. I tell you this because being a port city, you would not believe how few people understand how we make money in this town. And wherever there is money there's crime, as you are about to see.

Helpfully enough these five names are in order of seniority in the company. Perhaps Partridge thinks that the scale of the chisel means some bigwig is on the take. Or maybe this first name on the list, Michael Powell, is his worst enemy and he's on an elaborate ruse to muddy the waters and get him fired. You see how you need two brains to carry this stuff? That's why me and Betty work so well together. She sits on her ass thinking and I go out and get the information.

Don't get the wrong idea. Betty and Miss Cool are not sitting around doing their nails right now. Miss Cool might be, granted. But Betty is more likely checking the horse racing and laying odds at the turf. One day someone should start a newspaper just for that. Keep that in mind if you want to understand her well. She used to work in the police with me, although they wouldn't let her on the beat, she solved a few cases just by sitting on her ass and asking questions nobody else thought of.

I'm not the best brains of the outfit, but that's only because I have to go out into the world. If I could sit in the warm every day, I would be better at thinking. My stroke of genius on this matter was to start at the bottom of the list on the grounds that the person old Partridge least suspected would know something about what was going on. My challenge was to figure it out without anyone realising Partridge is the one pulling the strings. Which gives me-

"Mr Partridge, sir?" I asked. He was figuring out the paperwork with Miss Cool in the outer sanctum. They both looked up at me. His hand was hovering over her backside, so I saved him an embarrassment there. "Sir, would you be able to give me a cover story in case someone asks why I'm poking around? Can I be your new hire or something like that?"

"Christ no, I don't want anyone thinking a new hire is snooping around. Tell them you're writing a book about my life." My mouth drooped open at this. But I didn't say anything. If that's less suspicious than a new deckhand learning the ropes then this case is going to be interesting. "Yes, Mr Bird. That's the least suspicious thing you can say unless you're going to spend forty hours a week doing work for me for free just so you can ask ten minutes of questions after the shift?"

He did have a point about that.

"I've got it sir. I'm writing your memoirs, thank you very much."

And we watched him don his coat and hat. "Good luck," he said, and floated out.

Miss Cool glared at me, but I wasn't interested in talking at that moment. My head was filling with ideas and I had to take some notes before they all floated away.

# CHAPTER TWO

My first time at the docks in months. By the time I got there at eleven the fog had lifted. I'm not saying the sun was shining and I could feel the heat on my cheeks, but it wasn't foggy and there were streaks of blue between the clouds in the mainly steel sky. Take the small things, Betty says.

I had decided to lose the cigarettes and the hat, and the overcoat, and I made a big show out of my pencil and notepad. Today I was a writer, a thinker, a questioner, but not a detective. Any police or private dick would sniff me out a mile away, but by starting on the bottom rung of the Lord Line company, with a panel beater called Jimmy Southman, I figured I had time to ease into my new role as biographer of old Partridge. Perhaps it wouldn't sound as crazy to young Jim as it did to me.

"You're what!" was the first thing out of his mouth. He openly laughed in my face. "Why start with me?"

"We have to start somewhere, sonny. And to be honest I have a feeling that the work going on in here is more important than those managers over in those offices think it is, and that the true story of this amazing shipping line is happening right in front of ourselves as we stand here."

He scratched his head. "What do you want to know?"

"Well, to cut to it. I don't want some kind of slick thing that makes this out to be the best job since sliced bread. I want whatever passes for the truth in your own eyes. For example, what's old Partridge *really* like to work for?"

And that was it. It was like surfing off the top of the Hoover dam. Christ I couldn't keep up with the pencil act so I just figured I would commit to memory whatever this kid wanted to say.

I came to realise that although Jimmy didn't exactly love working here, it was broadly as good or bad as everywhere else. They got paid on time, although not enough. Nobody actually hurt them, at least not deliberately, and Jimmy was unaware of any serious injuries in the three years he had been hitting metal in this shed. What Jimmy was saying, in his own painfully slow and wordy way, is that there's nothing interesting to put in a book. Just some guys making boats in a shed that will one day carry other people's stuff around the world and back, and if everyone's lucky they never sink. End. *Finis.*

By the time I left that shed the blue streaks of sky had gone and the rain was coming down. I needed a drink.

I found a drink in the Black Boy, Ye Olde Black Boy no less. It's been in the same place for two hundred years and possibly much longer. They know me in there, so I sat quietly at my notes with what passes for whisky in that place. They don't sell bourbon for any price I can afford.

The question wasn't so much as why Jimmy was so bland and on the edges of interest to Partridge. The question was: why was he on the list at all?

This guy, a junior guy, had been around a couple of years bashing metal and riveting stuff together. An important job, without which the ships would fall apart. But Partridge's charge levelled against his own staff was that they were on the take in the cargo sense. They were somehow sliding off with some of the stock, not pulling from the till or driving off in a stolen ship. Jimmy had nothing to do with that side of the business at all.

In fact, now I came to reflect, it was not common for a single company to build the boats and manage them once they took to sea. Those two businesses were chalk and cheese. It was only the sheer scale of Partridge's Lord Line outfit that allowed him to exploit both sides of the business. My guess was that shipbuilding itself was low on margin. The big money came from the stock, and if you could get a huge contract, say a sugar contract or spices that could only be obtained in India or Asia then you could rake it in.

Lord Line are not into fishing trawlers, for example. I'd say you could care less about these things, these nuances, as the French say. But they will be important.

Fish are close by and plentiful, and they require smaller boats. These Lord Line ships are monsters. B-I-G. Big. They are some of the biggest ships on the entire seven seas. The ships look like a village has just rolled up out of the distance, wobbling all over and looking for land. They are like an alien invasion, that's how to think of it, when they arrive. The sailors and the supporting hands, the people who load and unload these things account for more than five in every hundred of every adult who lives in this town. So you need to know that fish is not sugar, which most people do. After that, you need to know that catching and storing fish for a few hours while you hightail it back to shore is not the game these boys are in. Longer, slower distances with longer, slower vessels. You could cream off a few sacks, even a few tonnes, of sugar or wood or steel and nobody would see it. A miscount here, a dropped oar there, and it's vanished into thin air. Jimmy, in this context, was not important. I struck him off the list and drained my glass. I asked for a bacon butty and returned to the docks.

I found Charlie Wilson in the next shed. He hadn't been around as long as Jimmy Southman and the two did not know each other very well, but they were aware of each other. They were people with skills, who *did* things, not managers sitting up there in the offices, daydreaming as they stared out to sea or up into space. They beat panels and carried loads and made ships that weren't quite ready into seaworthy craft. They both carried huge respect with me. Perhaps Mr Partridge had written out the first five names that came into his head, but I was still working on the more likely theory that the whole gig was a smoke screen.

"Morning, Charlie. They said it was all right to talk for five minutes."

"You're that writer guy?" Word was spreading fast.

"I'm Ted." I held out a hand, but Charlie held up his own, black with grease, and waved it instead.

"What do you want to know?"

"Just the basics. How long you've worked here, what you think of the managers, that sort of thing. If you have any funny or otherwise memorable stories, they might make it into the book."

We sat down on a row of girders or beams, and Charlie looked happy for an extra paid break. He was slightly out of breath as he recounted his story.

He had started working here a year ago and enjoyed the work, but he had grand ambitions and it seemed like they were as far away as ever and not getting closer. "Still," he said, "I'm impatient. I have thirty years ahead of me to plot my route to the boardroom."

It seemed unbelievable that someone starting here, lumping steel in these sheds, could ever aspire to become an executive.

"I know you're sceptical, and it's true that Partridge was born into management, but he was very junior when he started here. And Mr Powell, now there's a man to talk to. He really did start off in these sheds and they paid him to go to college and all that, and now look where he is. Right there up in the boardroom with Gelder, too."

You did hear of such things, but perhaps only because they were so rare. I considered that Powell, if this story was totally accurate, was a one-off, and indeed such a story would have made a book if one was ever written. Of those on my list we had Wilson and Southman representing the working man, Gelder and Powell representing the boardroom and then Pearson somewhere in the middle, caught between two stools. He was a manager, but he might well have started in the sheds after leaving school at a young age. They were a mixed bunch, and for a moment I wished that I was writing a book. They each would have interesting stories if only I had the time and patience to coax them out.

"How do you get on with young Jimmy Southman?"

"He's a good lad. We don't see each other much at work, but I see him sometimes in the pub on Fridays and Saturdays. He's an honest lad, but there are hundreds of us working out here. I keep a close circle, keep my head down, and try to look for a chance to progress."

"And you don't see anything unusual that might make a good yarn? This company seems to have a grand reputation with everyone in the town."

"Yes, they've been a fixture here for almost a hundred years, haven't they? There's no secrets for you to uncover. And if there was, old man Partridge would want them buried."

I looked at him. He didn't seem to be pulling a story now, he seemed genuinely to think there were no secrets here.

"Well, Charlie, thanks for your time. If you do hear of anything, something that might make a good chapter in the book, then the girls in reception know where to find me."

"Fine. Thanks for talking to me, it's always nice to have a rest. I'll get back to it."

# CHAPTER THREE

The good thing about this town is you can walk everywhere. Apart from the likes of Donald Partridge in his Anlaby country pile, everyone could walk to see everyone else. Perhaps the only reason the likes of Partridge live so far out west is to stop the likes of me asking tricky questions. Even the trams don't reach out there.

I decided to stroll by the office on the way to the name from the top of the list: Michael Powell, as Charlie Wilson had mentioned him. Mr Powell doesn't work in the factory or maintenance sheds, he's somehow involved in shipping the stuff around at a management level. I considered the possibility that Partridge had stuffed his prime target right in the middle of the list, and decided to keep it in mind for later. That would be a man called Pearson.

Betty was sheepishly returning the telephone to its cradle when I rolled up. "News report, Bird," she barked over the incessant hammering typewriter.

"No. 5 on the list is not of interest. A genuine red herring as far as my radar goes."

"What about the first four?"

"Charlie Wilson seemed innocent enough for now. I'll tell you more later. Any developments here?"

"You started at the bottom? You think Partridge is giving us the soft soap?" she asked, smiling.

"Of course he is."

"They always do, right Ted. Just what I was thinking. But they all do the soap in their own way. Is he on the take? Covering up and using us as an insurance policy?" I waited for her to continue. "I had a chat with our old friends at the station and they're not interested in Partridge. Not yet anyway. They spotted at once that he's not our usual bitter divorce type customer."

"Thanks, that's useful all the same. I'm off to chat to a Mr Powell. See you this afternoon."

Mr Powell was out, according to the receptionist, but she helpfully mentioned that Mr Gelder was in his office. He sat in the middle of a cloud of smoke, in conference with a couple of colleagues when I arrived. I felt like he was going to insist on my making an appointment. He hesitated just a moment when I gave the spiel about the book and took out my pencil. The other two were putting on their coats when I arrived anyway, which reduced his options for claiming to be busy.

"Thanks, sir," I said as he offered me a warm seat.

"Mr Partridge is writing his memoirs, is he?" asked Gelder in a way that made me think he was reading into it that Partridge was going to hand over the reins.

"He's not going anywhere, Mr Gelder. But time marches on for all of us."

He nodded and finally sat down, puffing on a pipe. I always thought there was something suspicious about a man who worked his way up to a pipe from cigarettes. They're social things, cigarettes, like a lighter or a bottle of whisky. A pipe is not for sharing.

"How long have you worked here, sir?" I started with the easy ones.

"Twenty years or more. It's the best shipping line in this city. As you might know, it's actually the only line that builds its own boats. There's no reason to leave this place unless you want to leave this industry, or leave the city for... warmer places."

"You can do that in this sort of place, I would imagine? Spread your wings. Contacts abroad."

"Yes of course. The influx of people makes this city what it is, but having that opportunity to go in the other direction is important too."

"Has anyone arrived recently? Earlier this year perhaps?"

"At the Lord Line?" He sucked on his pipe a while. "In the sheds certainly, yes, in the building and maintenance yards. The stevedores come and go on a daily basis. But not in the offices."

We went on like this for a bit. Then I got serious. "Mr Gelder, you know the sort of book that gets written about companies paid for by the managers, I imagine. Not very colourful. Mr Partridge wants us to get something of the real flavour. I don't want you to think we'll include anything controversial, mind. But can you remember a recent - say, in the last couple of years - a recent sort of event or notable occurrence, say?"

I hoped he liked my meandering way of putting it, trying to downplay it and yet emphasize it at the same time.

"Ah. There are so many little things, excitements that come up. But they are quickly forgotten. And anything that sticks in the memory is probably not what we want you printing!"

I smiled. He was a sharp one. He hadn't expected this conversation, remember. "Mr Gelder, I'm going to let you mull things over for a few days. Can you call me if anything jumps into your mind? Otherwise I'll come back on Friday, is that alright with you?"

He nodded. "Yes, it makes for something interesting leading into the weekend. It's been nice to be thought of by Mr Partridge. I'll give you a call the moment I think of something."

And that was it. But I wanted to return not only to Gelder here but to Jimmy too. Why hadn't I asked him about new arrivals? The more you work a case, the more possibilities start to jump out. It wasn't only Gelder that had some thinking to do. He was being overly helpful to my mind.

That was when I threw the script out the window. This wasn't detective work. Clients who can give you a list of five names can give you a list of twenty. And clients with a true list of only five names, with the resources available on Partridge's own payroll didn't need me. I'm letting the idea of a proper conversation with Partridge at his pretty little home simmer on the back burner for a while. But he sure as hell is setting us up, leading us along breadcrumbs towards some end point he already understands the shape of. It could be dangerous, although knowingly putting us in danger might be a bigger problem for him. He doesn't know Betty like I do. But whatever is really going on at Lord Line is not with the five on this list. I threw the list in the bin, then I put it back on the desk and grabbed my coat. I was going to do what I do best: talking and drinking. I'm going to listen to the public rumour mill about Lord Line and see what lands on my dock.

Ethel was hot stuff. I hadn't seen her in a couple of months but she spotted me first. I was adjusting my hat on the stand when she touched my arm.

"Hello, Edward," she said. "Buy me a drink." It wasn't a question. She was a cute little trick and nobody ever turned her down. A nod from me secured two beers and two gin slings for Ethel. We sat at the bar where both of us could admire her reflection in the mirror behind the bottles.

"I hear you're on a case," she said after an initial slurp.

"I'm always on a case."

"There's almost nothing going on here that I don't know something about," she said modestly.

"I'm under orders. Discretion required."

"Pish!" She slurped again. At this rate she'd need another before we got going. She grabbed my knee and smiled, then lit up a filterless thing on a stick. "You don't come in a place like this to sit silently in the corner. Cut to it, brother."

"What can you say about the Lord Line?"

She stopped slurping. "What can I say about the largest line in town? The most prestigious? My God, where do I start? They have more enemies than friends."

"Why is that?"

She waved her hand around as if clearing smoke. "Jealousy, envy, other sins. Greed. Failure. Pride. You need to give me a little more, Ted."

"Someone thinks that someone else is chiselling some product out of thin air and possibly cooking the books to hide it."

"Pish! Some white collar stuff. Who cares? Nobody's going to die."

"That's what I thought, but that's how these things always start. Once I start kicking tyres, that's when people start getting hot and shooting each other."

Ethel continued slurping and smoking and looking at her reflection. I reached for my wallet, the only way to speed this up. I had to get over to Partridge's mansion before dusk or Ethel would start taking advantage of me. I slipped a couple of notes out and looked meaningfully at Ethel.

"Is Partridge involved?" she asked.

I nodded. "Know him?" She hit my leg, pretty hard.

"Not like that. Not like you. Forget him, he's as dull and straight as you would expect. I think he's a Quaker. You're working for him?"

I nodded again. "You're fast, Ethel. With that kind of speed of thought you might not need another gin."

That got me another hit on the leg.

"If you hurry up and give me those notes I'll let you know that you're barking at the wrong dog."

"If you want either of these notes you need to tell me more than that. Which dog barks?"

"Ask the bitch, not the dog."

"The woman? What woman?"

"Partridge's woman. Start with her and don't move on until you've exhausted all avenues."

"Thanks Ethel. I'm heading over there now. Here's the two notes. Don't drink it all at once. I'm over to Partridge's now so I can be back before dusk and the highwaymen on the road to Anlaby."

She laughed at that. "Highwaymen! I'd pay for that kind of Dick. This is the modern day, Ted. Highwaymen in Kingstown!"

The journey out west was easy enough. I arrived in Anlaby at three of the clock, which gave me an hour or so to play around before dusk.

The bus pulls up outside the Red Lion pub, just before you get to the church. I didn't want to take the next stop in case I was seen before I had a chance to patrol the area. Partridge lives at South Ella Hall, which is exactly how it sounds. Billiard room, library, croquet, the whole shooting match. Plus shooting grouse at the right time of year. There were two lodges to choose from, which further helps set the scene, and the nearest was a five minute walk. It's the kind of place you're supposed to arrive by coach and four horses, breezing through the gates as they are still opening as if automatically. They would frown upon foot passengers, but so be it.

"Appointment?" said the porter, looking at my feet and then my knees. "You walked?"

"Yes I walked and yes I have an appointment with the gentleman at the hall, sir."

"Name?"

"Bird."

"Really, sir?"

"Yes."

"No Bird on my list."

"Then call up to the house."

I paced up and down while he sorted things out. Ethel's advice made me hope that Partridge was out, due home around five-thirty, perhaps. But if he was out, who would vouch for me?

"Would you like me to arrange a coach for you, sir? The lady of the house said you can wait in the drawing room until Mr Partridge arrives home."

I nodded as if this was the expected answer.

When I said the house is as you would expect, it's not. It's far grander. I had checked the maps and done my preparatory perambulations but still my mouth hung a little loose as the gig bobbed along behind a single horse.

Sometimes it's the funny little things you notice that become important. I happened to see that under the horse's rear axle was a cloth square stretched out at just the right tension to catch any doings that might emerge from the animal's back end. This would save untold hours scraping the stuff off the stony driveway.

Engines were on the way, of course they were, and no doubt it was the motor car that transported Partridge to the docks each morning, but this is the way to arrive at a grand house. The front door swung open as the horse drew up and I swept into the lobby as though I owned the joint. The butler nodded to a door, the drawing room, and I slid through it, finding myself a chair near the bay window with a view over the darkening lawn.

Someone brought me a drink, a scotch and water. I sipped, surveying the grounds. I sensed movement behind me, but nobody spoke. I didn't turn around.

"Good afternoon, Bird," said a thin, crystal glass voice that had to be Mrs Partridge. I turned slowly. My God. She was wearing a low evening dress and tiara. Some kind of mink-looking tail wrapped around her neck and heels. The dress was black and had diamonds or some such sparkling from its full extent.

"Going out, madam?" I sensed one of my eyebrows was raised involuntarily.

"We're hosting," she replied. "You want Partridge?"

"I had hoped for a gentle confab with the gentleman of the house, yes."

"Then you've a wait on your hands. Expecting you, was he?"

She slide over to the sideboard and began working up a drink. There were two glasses.

"I hadn't booked, Mrs Partridge, I admit. Normally my clients like to make time for me, to check that their money is going in the right places."

"Call me Lana. Can I help?"

I shrugged. "Maybe."

"Ask away."

Ethel's advice began to come back to front of mind. Start with the bitch. But this wasn't the sort of bitch I expected. This was Crufts top show. I began to vocalise my thoughts, something that came naturally to me.

"I'm working for your husband. He's publishing a book about the history of the Lord Line."

She openly scoffed at that. "Quit the veneer, Bird. I know all about you."

"He has some evidence, or at any rate, suspicion, that one or more of his men are on the chisel. They are secretly, and very expertly, taking merchandise off his boats and hiding it in the paperwork somehow, to cover their tracks. I have a list of five names and I've spoken to three of the men today. I'd like to make a report to Mr Partridge to see what his reaction is."

"That's all very carefully worded. Show me the names."

I certainly hesitated, but handed her the moist and crumpled slip from my pocket. She glanced at it and passed it back.

"You spoke to Charlie Wilson," she stated, no question mark. Why choose him? He was number four.

"I did as it happens."

"Waste of time, it's not him."

"Perhaps that's why he's near the bottom. Any other names jump out?"

"I think you're on a goose chase, Mr Bird."

"Did your old- did Mr Partridge express any of his concerns to you?"

"He did not and if he had I'd have told him he was wasting his time. Everyone's on the take, Bird. As long as it's not hurting anyone, why follow it up? You might not like where it all leads."

"I might not like it?"

"I was speaking generally. Mankind might not like too much truth. Have another drink."

I started sipping even more gingerly. I wished Ethel had been more specific. I wished Partridge had been home.

"Are you close to your husband, madam?"

She snorted. "What kind of question is that! He's *not* my *husband*." She said it as though she was describing a slug on her stiletto. I felt relieved. He had to be thirty years older than her.

"I meant, would it be normal for him to discuss any work trouble at home?"

"No it would not. I only heard about you from the housekeeper, as if by accident. I am sure she did it deliberately. She must have heard from the butler."

"I see. But this lack of disclosure would not be seen as abnormal in any way?"

She shook her head and emptied her glass, then wistfully took herself off for another. She got another two clean glasses out even though mine was untouched.

"It's going to be quite a party tonight," I said, and sipped again.

"You should stay for it, if you can find something to wear. You might learn something more than these pointless questions." She looked at me again, then shouted for the butler. He must have been waiting at the door to arrive that quickly.

"Archer, get this man into some evening wear. There's a man living here about his size. And now excuse me, Mr Bird. I will attend to the final preparations while you get dressed with Archer here."

And she was gone.

# CHAPTER FOUR

The party. Old man Partridge had arrived home quietly and without fanfare. The first I knew of his return was when I spotted him across the ballroom in a fog of cigarette smoke. He didn't see me at first, so I strolled in his direction, looking away, and then turned my head as I hoved within thirty feet. He nodded and tipped his glass towards me. I nodded, and that was it. Some detectives call that card marking. He knows I'm here and I know he knows. No more than that. The questions would come later.

I cast my eye around the room, suddenly aware I was wearing Partridge's second dinner suit. I shrugged. He wasn't about my size at all and I felt like a child in dress-up. I had made an extra hole in his belt with a nail I recovered from a doorframe using pliers supplied by a gardener. I spied Gelder by the punch bowl. I doubted the ship's lad I spoke to in the repair shed would be invited. I strode over to Gelder, all smiles.

"Good evening, Mr Gelder."

He looked momentarily confused, just a brief flash before he smiled. "Mr Bird! Good to see you. Here, grab a glass. The punch is great here, I just love fruit and alcohol."

"I didn't take you for a drinker, sir."

"Just on the odd occasion, of course. Social drinking. It's really all part of the job."

"Is you wife here?"

He nodded. "I lost her pretty quickly. She doesn't get along..."

"With Lana? I'm not surprised at all, I hear that's a common feeling."

Gelder smiled and gulped at his drink. "You're not married, Bird?"

"Once. A long time ago. Didn't have the time, or the money."

Gelder gave me a look of envy. "Well, Mr Bird, there are one or two eligible young ladies available for a dance later on. Keep an eye."

I nodded as he retreated to find his better half. The problem with this set is, most of all, the class rules that still apply, even after a terrible war that looks likely to be repeated with even heavier weapons. They're so tightly bound by some unwritten set of expectations that they become puppets. The only thing worse than the class rules, of course, is not having any rules. Even we 'biographers' have to observe certain social niceties. It would all be much easier just to bash a crystal glass and bellow at the whole lot of them, but who would admit to theft in such an environment? It was an amusing thought.

"Hello, Bird. What do you know?"

Partridge had sloped over. "I think Gelder is in the clear," I replied. "And that boy in the repair shed."

Partridge nodded. "You started at the bottom. Good man! I don't suppose you've ruled me out, old sport?"

I smiled at that one. "I take nothing at face value, sir, except that he who pays the bill calls the tune."

"Fair enough, Bird. Funny that you're here, actually. I passed by your office on the way home and beckoned your boss over for drinks. Don't know why I didn't think of it sooner. She might be more relaxed at this kind of bash than you, and, well-"

I raised my hand. "No offence, sir. All's well." The truth, I imagined, was that Partridge had no such idea and that Betty had engineered the whole show once she found out, no doubt through either Ethel or Miss Cool, that I had sallied into the devil's lair without invitation. No sooner had Partridge melted away than I spied Betty driving towards me, a glass in each hand and a broad smile across her face. She swooped her arm around my shoulder, slipped a glass into my hand and pecked me on the cheek all in one graceful glide.

"What do you know?" she asked with a wink.

"Nothing at all, which is why I'm here. I wanted a quiet chat with Partridge. I didn't know all these people would swing past for a party. But that might be useful somehow."

"It certainly will."

"You knew I was here. Do you have a message?"

Betty nodded. "Ethel had a word. She's a cute trick. I didn't think much of our client's little list and she confirmed my suspicions."

"About two hours after she confirmed mine," I replied. "Why don't you go and use your femininities on the men?"

"Mr Partridge-"

"I said the men. He's up to his neck in something and he's using us for cover. Either Gelder over there is involved or he isn't. My guess is that anyone on the list is in the clear, but I wouldn't mind a second opinion."

Betty smiled and drifted Gelder's way. I scanned the room. I wouldn't mind another round with Lana Partridge. I saw her. "Are you enjoying yourself, Bird?" she asked.

"I'm working, madam."

"There are certain occupations where the two things inevitably merge, Bird. May I call you Edward?"

I nodded. She continued. "You're on call each and every day, every hour. You're like a Victorian pieceworker, taking your work home with you. Always ready to drop whichever lady you're striding around with. Danger on every corner. God, it sounds great to me."

"Are you close to Mr Partridge?"

She smiled. "You asked me that earlier and I didn't give you a proper answer. Do you have eyes, Bird?"

"Mine are unusually effective. I can see through things. I can see what isn't there."

"Essential in your line of work. Then you don't require a verbal answer. He has money and I have youth. That's the be-all."

"Care for a punch?"

"You're funny, Mr Bird. It's my grandmother's recipe. I will allow you to walk me to the bowl."

Hell, she could dance. It was impossible to gap with her, even for appearance's sake. She went all in. I sensed a few turned heads, but not enough to cause a stir. Partridge was nowhere. She insisted on a tango, my weak suit for more than one reason. She grinded around like a dervish. There was a glisten on her brow, colour in her cheeks. I wished there was a rose for her mouth. I knew Betty was watching, somewhere, and I desperately tried to escape. This woman was dangerous. Suddenly I felt an arm at my elbow, pulling me away.

"Edward, a word. Sorry, Mrs... I'll bring him back."

Betty spoke in hushed tones. "Gelder is a fool. He's either the only actor in this town yet to be recognised by the Academy or he's a fool. I'm going home. Let's meet at nine in the office. I can see you're making ground with the good lady. Looking at you two, I think she's involved in whatever this is and she's softening you up. Be gone from here before midnight and don't drink anything."

"Good night, mother," I said, but with a wink. When I turned around, Lana had two more punches and she was gulping at hers like it was iced water on a hot summer day.

"Could we try something slower?" I said and sipped gingerly. This was too much temptation to take for my first night on the job.

It was tough getting into the office for nine when I knew Betty hadn't made such a time in history. But it would be nice making a drink for Miss Cool. My hands wobbled a little from booze and it would do me good.

"Good morning, Miss Cool. Are you ready for coffee?"

She nodded, but she wasn't rattling the keys this morning. The urgent work was over for another week. There was no urgency on a Tuesday. She had a notepad and a cigarette, and she watched me grind the beans, and don't ask where we get those.

"How is the case?" she asked.

"Early days. You never liked Partridge and neither does anyone else, especially his wife. He's a fool, in a sense, but he knows the score. He doesn't care. He doesn't need or want children."

"He already has a family. They're all grown up."

"That so?"

"I, er, happen to know his son. The younger son."

"Now is that so?" I thought that over. "Not with the current lady of the house, he doesn't. My God, his sons would be her age."

Miss Cool smiled. "That's what I thought too."

"Can you take over at the grinder, Miss Cool? I need to make a call."

It didn't take me a minute to pull the former Mrs Partridge out of the telephone directory. She must have a pretty penny herself. Probably lived out in Anlaby with the other hoi polloi. I dialled. And who should answer? That's right, it was Mr Gelder. I decided to pay his home a visit after he had left for work. I didn't say anything, just hung up, and grabbed my coat. It was not nine yet and he must be getting his coat on too.

I kissed Miss Cool on the forehead as I darted out towards the door. "Thank you, Miss Cool. You can update Betty for me. The future Mrs Partridge is in something up to her eyes, I just don't know what. I didn't drink and I left at ten minutes to midnight. Good morning, Miss Cool."

She smiled and started boiling some water.

That was how I found myself in Anlaby just a few short hours after I left the place. Mr Gelder's house at Anlaby Manor stood detached in its own grounds with a high wall around the garden, but otherwise it was open to the street. There might have been a carriage entrance to the rear, but the front was reached on foot. I pushed through the squeaky gate and strode up to the front door. A butler answered.

"Good morning, I'd like a quick word with Mrs - with the lady of the house, please."

"Right you are, sir. Follow me into the drawing room and I'll see if she's home."

It was approaching ten o'clock which meant two things. She would certainly not have left for any engagements, and she would be fully dressed. Any delay would therefore tend me towards suspicion. I reflected in that idle moment on how Miss Cool seemed to be well-connected to this set and wondered whether I could make more use of her in the field.

"Good morning," said Mrs Partridge, perhaps hesitantly. Perhaps my arrival was a complete surprise, but I didn't think so.

"Good morning, madam," I stated, trying to avoid using any name for her which might trip me up. I was sure as hell she wasn't Mrs Gelder yet, but had no clue as to how she labelled herself.

"We were not expecting you," she said. "Are you here for Alfred? He's left for work already."

"I've been asked to investigate a small matter for Mr Partridge," I said. Would she already know? Should I try that rot about the book?

"You don't need to start in with all that guff about writing a book. You must be Edward. I'd heard about you."

"From whom, may I ask?"

"Actually from two sources. You're gaining notoriety. Alfred mentioned some rubbish about a book but I also heard about you at the party last night. I recognise you."

Yes! She had been at the party. There had been too many people to talk to everyone. Ted didn't remember seeing her in the same frame as Gelder or Mr Partridge. Diplomacy, possibly. Or perhaps she didn't like him.

"Are you here to question me, Mr Bird?"

"Certainly not, madam-"

"Oh call me Eileen, please. You can't decide whether it's Mrs Gelder or Mrs Partridge and if we're going to be honest with each other, neither can I. I never liked Miss Ramsbottom, even as a child, for obvious reasons. Eileen will do."

Luckily the butler saved me from a quick reply and I requested a cup of tea. Using that time for thinking, I decided to open the bowling gently. "Eileen, thank you. I'm not here on any specific errand, I admit. I am at a very early stage in proceedings. I might as well ask you directly. Are you aware much of what goes on at the docks, in the offices of the Lord Line?"

She shook her head. "If I were I would most probably still be resolutely Mrs Partridge, Mr Bird. They shut me out of the show completely. They leave before dawn and return at all hours, then they tell me virtually nothing about what they've been doing. It might not surprise you to hear that Mr Gelder is just as secretive as Mr Partridge, so I'm rather feeling I've made a terrible decision. Well, there you are. The lot of the woman. I can't tell you anything."

"On the contrary, Eileen. That is very useful. Have they been spending more time at the office of late than previously? I wonder if things are not as rosy as advertised. Perhaps they're dealing with a crisis?"

"No, that's not it. They've always worked like dogs. They share the trappings as carefully as they can. The wives get to sit in nice houses and take each other out for tea, but I have nothing else to entertain me. It should be clear that the newer model Mr Partridge has installed is not married to him and is of a rather different generation to myself, so we don't see each other. The other wives are my age, if you'll forgive me considering such an indelicate matter at this hour. We get along all right, but only in the way you might get along with a colleague. Nobody shared anything, you see, as it will make its way back to the husbands."

She flopped into an armchair and looked a little desperate. There was only one thing to do. "Mrs - Eileen. I have a capital idea."

I took Eileen out for lunch. There are a number of passable tea rooms in Anlaby, a short walk from her house, and I could expense it through Partridge although I wouldn't admit to it.

"Welsh rarebit, pot of tea, French fancies," she rattled off like a gun. I wasn't really interested so asked for the same. She didn't need to look at the menu, either.

"I didn't have you down for French fancies," she said. "They're usually pink."

"Sugar's sugar, madam. I don't mean to pry, Eileen," I started off. Anyone who has ever said that always uses it to cover a prying approach. "I'm very sorry that you're having difficulties with Mr Partridge. I have an eye for these things and I'm working quite closely with him. Would you like me to say anything that might... smooth things over?"

"There is nothing you could say. Time might heal, but I doubt it. He's going off the rails, I fear."

"But if an opportunity did arise, is it something you would seek? Or is Mr Gelder..."

Luckily the rarebits arrived. She looked thoughtful as she stuffed big chunks into her cavernous hole. "That is a very good question, Mr Bird."

I decided to eat. Silence can elicit the most profound information. Eventually, she continued. "I'm afraid I don't care much for either of them."

"A difficult situation," I admitted. It wasn't easy being a middle class female, and Mrs Partridge was several rungs above that. The trouble was that the system squashed all personality out of them. To compare Eileen to Ethel was a harsh thing to do. They were different species. But a man like Partridge wouldn't know how to relate to Ethel the barfly. Were I to compare Ethel to the new model Mr Partridge had installed, the comparison would be more polite. In other words, I had a distinct impression that the new model was new money. Very new. I sensed that Mr Partridge had elevated her considerably and she was struggling to adapt. And how had Ethel known about *that* situation?

"Eileen, I just had an idea."

She stuffed the final chunk of rarebit down and slurped at her tea. She looked up. "Which is?"

"I'll pick you up at seven tonight. Be ready outside the house. I'll come with transport. This is work. If anyone asks, and only if they ask, tell them you're doing an interview for the old man's book."

# CHAPTER FIVE

"The wanderer returns!" exclaimed Betty as I strolled in around three o'clock. Miss Cool was putting her coat on. Something about a tooth. Betty gestured me into her office.

"Our client has made a complaint about your conduct," she said, but not unkindly. This would be interesting. Betty waved to Miss Cool through the frosted glass, and I saw a vague shape that might have been waving back.

"Does he disagree with my approach?"

"Yes he does. He gave you a list of five names, of which you spoke to three, starting with the last two, not the first two. Then you get yourself invited to free punch and spend too long with his current piece. Then - for added comprehensiveness - you take his former piece, the actual Mrs Partridge, out to lunch! Am I to grasp that the lunch was on expenses?"

"It was a business meeting," I stated.

"Indeed!"

"Look, we're on fixed price. Nobody set a deadline."

"I did. You said something like, oh, it'll take a week?"

"That was my guess at that point, true. But it's not a deadline. Partridge never asked us to wrap it up in a week - that was your suggestion. And further information has come to light."

"I should hope it has, Bird! We're two days in now."

Betty was always watching the clock. You could understand it if we had more work than we could handle, but that happy event had arisen just once in our year together in private practice. Our first twenty years together in the police seemed overjoyed with the burden of work. It was like night and day. Only this time, we got paid for all the hours we worked and if there wasn't enough work we didn't have to pretend to look busy, although Betty tried to keep us honest.

"Give me your theory, Ted, and do it in short words."

"I don't have one." Betty narrowed her eyes. "Not after two days of meet and greets. And red herrings and lies. I don't have a theory, not yet. It's one of two things, probably. Either he sent us to his friends, having tipped them off, which means he's doing a kind of smokescreen pretence of investigating whatever is going on. This gives him the ability to say he looked into whatever he heard on the grapevine and there was nothing to it. In that instance, he's the kingpin and he's lying out his ass. The other possibility is that someone is getting close to the throne, most likely the top one or two names on the list, and he wants us to put the heat on them, scare them into a mistake, and then he can fire them without contradiction to protect his position for the next ten years. That will see him out."

"I pretty much got all this myself, Ted."

"The second option would explain why he's mad as hell I haven't approached the top name on the list yet."

"It would."

"But there is a third option and one that I consider the most likely." Betty nodded and explored her teeth with a pencil, so I continued. "Partridge hasn't got the first clue what's going on. He's genuinely mystified, curious as hell, and scared. He's totally genuine and on the level. That would explain why he jumped at your fixed price offer."

"My offer was conditional on you solving the case after five conversations, Bird." She stood, rising to her full five feet. "Now get out there and talk to the top name on the list pronto. I will call Partridge to inform him about our next course of action. I want a theory tomorrow, Ted."

Eileen Partridge was standing at the bus stop in Anlaby when my cab pulled up. I opened the door for her, and we sped off back to town.

I chose my regular bar, expecting to find Ethel. She always seemed to be there when I wanted a drink. Perhaps she was always here, or perhaps I always fancied a drink. It was time to shake the tree. Shaking the tree always tended to make the ripe fruit fall to the floor.

Ethel's curiosity about Eileen would be so unbearable, I expected her to intercept us before he removed his hat.

"Good evening, sailor!" shouted Ethel across the bar as we entered. I nodded, and tried to fill my eyes with a warning: give us five minutes to settle in. Ethel wasn't used to picking up on such signals over thirty feet away and she rolled over.

"Good evening, Ethel. Pleased to introduce Eileen, whom I am interviewing for my book."

"Ah, that *book*," repeated Ethel, signalling at last that she had tuned into the correct wavelength. "Welcome, Eileen. We are all friends here. I trust the interview won't get in the way of a good chinwag?"

"Certainly not!" exclaimed Eileen. "I'll have what you're having, here's some money and get Mr Bird something."

After Ethel had departed clutching a large note, Eileen turned to me. "She's quite a catch, Mr Bird. Let's not spoil a good evening with talk of that godawful book, shall we? Are you still on platonic terms with the good lady?"

"Indeed I am!" I almost dropped my coat as I perched it on the stand. "Eileen and I have a certain professional overlap and we've known each other since the war."

"Pish! Get on with it, boy. Life's short, believe me. Now, should we sit or stand, or take one of those tall stools?"

The evening proceeded broadly as you might imagine, and I called a cab at ten thirty to convey Eileen home. I decided she would be better travelling alone, which gave me an opportunity to debrief Ethel. As I expected, they had taken a couple of walks to the lavatories together and I surmised those walks would be the highlights of any information Eileen had let slip.

Ethel explained that the current living arrangements of the Partridges was quite recent, perhaps of six months' duration. Mrs Partridge, now living with Alfred Gelder, had found her presence unnecessary, in her husband's eyes, and he had installed a much younger woman, the iridescent Lana, in her place at the hall. Although it might seem a rush to the outsider, Mrs Partridge hadn't been content with her husband since a few weeks after their honeymoon, which was so long ago that nobody could recall the year.

"Thank you, Ethel. Anything else?"

She shook her head, and I paid for another drink before leaving.

What do I know about accounts and paperwork? One of Partridge's complaints had been that whoever was stealing from him was covering their trail with false paperwork. The trouble was, even if I was looking at false paperwork I wouldn't know how to interpret it. I didn't trust Partridge to give out anything like the full story: any request to see the files would be met with evasion.

"Miss Cool, one moment please?"

Nightfall discovered Miss Cool and I hiding in the shadows beside a hole in the fence at the docks. The Lord Line building was an art deco oblong stuck onto the headland by the estuary. An estuary might sound fancy but it just means the part of a river that meets the sea. For a shipping company, a tidal estuary as wide and deep as this one was like the gold rush. Direct access to the rest of the world. The building always seemed to me like a grounded ship, grinding its gears eastwards and wondering why it wasn't moving. I knew why I wasn't moving. We didn't know anything about security arrangements at the company. We were late enough that most of the windows were in darkness, but not so late that the security guards would be getting bored and looking for a nap. I sensed Miss Cool's natural poise waning.

"Mr Partridge would have just shown you the paperwork, Ted," she observed, folding her arms tight around her body and shivering.

"Assumption one is that he's not on the level. He might have already cleaned out any dodgy files but we don't want to give him another chance. If there's anything still in there of value, we need to find it tonight. Assumption two is that he wouldn't expect to be robbed by me, and he therefore likely has not cleaned out his filing cabinets."

"You're sure that Partridge himself is in something up to his neck?"

I nodded. We were going to proceed on our wits. On my wits. I pulled back the fencing wire to make the hole a little bigger. "After you," I said, and gestured towards the low gap. Miss Cool proceeded without complaint. At least we were moving.

We strode rapidly across the scrubland around the office. There were no lights around the outside and our shared torch was firmly off until we arrived inside. With only a fine sliver of moon to light us, I felt confident but we walked fast. I wanted no record of our visit so I had already discounted the idea of blagging past the front desk. Once we reached the shadow of the main building, we proceeded slowly. Every drain pipe, every window might provide a point of entry. In a building this size, someone always left a window open, in even in winter. The heating was always too hot for someone, the air too rank, the lure of a window catch impossible to resist. I'll open it just a crack. Only one out of the five hundred or so staff would need that thought and we would be in.

I saw what I needed but it was three floors up. I could just about see my way via a drainpipe and a ledge, but even Miss Cool looked concerned when she followed my gaze upwards. "Don't worry. We'll find a side door. Wait for me at the side door. I will open it from the inside but I'll need the torch."

And that was how we got in.

The bigger question for me was never about getting in. What were we looking for and how would we know it when we saw it? That was the reason for dragging Miss Cool along. Her life so far, although shorter than mine by a considerable margin, had been spent among paper. She intuitively grasped its meaning from a single glance. Bill, invoice, archive, record, letter. She could process a filing cabinet inside half an hour, I was sure. A great help to us, and something for you to reference for the future, is that large office buildings are always signposted. Those wooden or plastic signs hang from the ceiling in every corridor of every office I have ever seen. I allowed Miss Cool to activate the torch.

"Let's go," I said, and strode off to look for signs. "Just listen for feet and we'll be fine."

On balance, the archives were likely to be on the ground floor or basement, if there was a basement this close to the river. In an office everything is about saving time, which is also called money to the people who live here during the working week. Lugging filing cabinets in and out of rickety lifts is not efficient. And filing cabinets don't need windows. Save them for the humans. On this basis we discovered that there was a basement, which also meant our torch wouldn't be spraying its light for two miles in every direction. We descended to the room of interest.

"I'll stand look out and listen for feet. You start from the first drawer."

"What are we looking for?" she asked, not unreasonably.

"Anything that grabs your attention. Try to find the drawers that record what goes on and off the ships."

"Like bills of lading?" she said. I covered my gaping jaw in the darkness. "They're over in the corner where it says bills of lading."

"Great, let's start."

We were out of that room inside half an hour. Miss Cool was clutching some likely-looking documents. For some reason, the fear got to me once we had finished. It was an easy matter to locate the exit and stride out into the open. Whatever happened after that could be explained with some fast talking now that we had some evidence. We wouldn't know if the documents were any good until we arrived back at base. No need for the drain pipe on the way out. We pushed through the door, shoved it shut, and walked home. Or, for the record, I saw Miss Cool to the end of her street, said she should have a lie in tomorrow, and I walked home holding the documents, keen to start work. It was one o'clock.

It was getting on for four o'clock when I found something, yawned, and went to bed in my clothes. Of the hundred or so sheets chosen by Miss Cool out of thousands in that room, she had chosen from the previous financial year, presumably to avoid detection. This in itself showed a level of cunning that surprised me. I could detect no importance in most of the sheets, and set those to one side. A small handful of documents were direct duplicates or safety copies done on carbon paper. I set those aside too. What was left was interesting. Not duplicates exactly, but nearly. Typed, not on carbon, were double copies of certain bills of lading. The only differences, impossible to detect at a glance, were in some of the numbers. A zero added or removed, a 1 became a 2 or 3. Identical copies except for a small selection of numbers. Forgeries. One for you, one for me. You assume yours is the same as mine, but it's not. One is for the tax and customs offices, one is for the management. One copy consistently understated the cargo, the other copy presumably reflected the actual cargo. I arranged them into two piles. One from each I folded into my jacket for Betty tomorrow, the rest I stored securely under a loose floorboard under a lightweight drawer unit which I then positioned on top of the hidden documents.

Night night.

# CHAPTER SIX

I wasn't ready for the office next morning, but I hauled in by nine. No Miss Cool, so I made sure to have Betty's coffee ready and hot when she arrived. Not boiled too early or too late. I slipped it into her hand as she walked past me, and followed her into the office, talking first to keep her calm.

"Miss Cool will be in later, Betty. Something about a tooth."

"A tooth you say? She didn't mention that on the stairs just now. She had to pick up some stationery items is the story she gave me."

"We have a breakthrough on the Partridge case," I ran on.

"About time! Sit down and tell me about it."

I told her about the duplicate bills of lading and the edited numbers. My assumption was that one copy was a forgery intended to hide something, no doubt for commercial advantage.

Betty glanced at the two documents side by side on her desk. "I wonder what Partridge will make of these?" she said, thoughtfully, looking directly at me.

"We can't show them to him. Not yet."

"Who gave them to you?"

"A source."

"Is it better that I don't know?"

I nodded, hoping Miss Cool hadn't said anything more on the stairs.

Betty turned to stare out of the window. "Are we going to make any money on this show?" she asked, as if to herself.

"I'm working on that angle. The fixed price thing is out of the window if we've been sold a dummy, of course. But I know how much you enjoy cake, Betty. If you give me another day I can square things off nicely on the money side."

"Normally you're not the numbers boy," she said, a little unkindly.

"My sources are assisting on the counting front."

"Right. Get out of here. Just do whatever it is as quick as you can."

I discovered Miss Cool ascending the stairs with some envelopes. She spoke first. "Did you find those duplicate bills of lading, Ted? The forgeries I mean."

"You knew about those? I was up until four looking at them."

"You should have mentioned it, I thought you would wait until this morning. The duplicates were in a different drawer, low down and unmarked. Did you see I took old ones so they wouldn't find anything missing? This has been going on a long time."

"Yes, it has, Miss Cool. The question is why is it coming to a head now? And why are we involved?"

"I'm sure you're off to find out."

I was. I just needed some quiet time to consider who to approach first. An original thought struck me quite firmly. I would go to the middle name, the third man, on Partridge's list. Who was that?

Pearson lived out north, for some inexplicable reason. The town was unusual in not having a south side, due to the estuary. The west was up and coming, and nearer to civilisation. The east was good farmland but led only to the sea. North would eventually take you to Scotland, but I was only heading out to Driffield. A small market town, tidy and often overlooked. Pearson was not part of the Anlaby set. Perhaps he had chosen the north to get away from them all. It seemed logical to me. An outcast. I would visit him after work, as the strategy had paid off handsomely with Partridge. If I timed my arrival just prior to the husband's, I would get twenty minutes alone with his wife. Until then, I would run some enquiries around the Lord Line offices with people other than Pearson to see what they felt about him. This was the kind of conversation where that old sop about writing a memoir would help. It would also serve the purpose of finding out whether the burglary last night had been noticed. I felt it unlikely.

As I walked through the main gates at Lord Line, it struck me that I only ever came here in fog or darkness and, on this occasion, in heavy rain. It was an isolated spot, not that convenient for the town centre bars and other attractions. It had a sort of Quaker tranquillity to the place, completely at odds with the under the counter shenanigans which were unfolding. It felt like someone was defrauding the church. Very poor form.

I decided that the full frontal assault on the receptionist would be worth a go.

"Yes, I'm writing a history of the firm, that's it. I'd like to talk to a colleague of Mr Pearson if possible, then I'll come back tomorrow to talk to him. Should I make an appointment for him now?"

"Yes, it's worthwhile. I'd heard about you. All very exciting."

"Well, to me a book's a book like any other, you see. But for some reason the companies I write about do seem to get rather giddy about matters."

"I've found you a slot with Mr Pearson at ten tomorrow. Let me just dial through and see if any of his colleagues want to chat to you. Take a seat, Mr Bird."

I didn't need to wait long. She had three volunteers lined up in a jiffy. "That was quick work, thank you. Should I walk through? I'm good about directions."

"No need. They're tightening up a few things. Mr Wong is coming down to collect you, then you can walk with him and ask your questions."

"Why are they tightening up?"

"Just general reasons. We don't get many visitors out here whom we don't know. It's out of the way."

"Thank you. And here's Mr Wong."

I can tell you that the three volunteers were complete time wasters from the point of view of the investigation. Had I been writing a book they had some dull anecdotes that could have filled a page or two. The thing about workplaces is that the rumours and gossip seem endlessly fascinating if you work there and agonisingly dull if you don't. The kind of book Partridge imagined would be a marketing exercise at best, sent free to key customers at Christmas. Staff would be forced to read a copy. The only surprise was that he hadn't done it for real.

I reeled out of there for a late lunch in town. The rain had stopped so I walked into marketplace and found a pub I hadn't seen for several weeks. Far enough from Partridge and Betty, and there was little chance of Ethel staggering in. I wanted a quiet meal for one and they put me on a stool in the window.

I started to feel the pressure of time. We could easily get out of the fixed price thing because it was founded on lies. But the only way to expose the lies at the moment was to admit to the burglary, or come up with a cover story that might be rumbled. So I had to find some other excuse before the money ran out. That would be the point at which Betty lost it and started making rash decisions. I had two more days, probably, before things got difficult. How to spend this afternoon? I ordered another beer. I had to crack this one, preferably using what I already knew.

Why had Partridge chosen to involve an outside agency? And why us? We'd had no prior dealings with him, having been in private business only a year. Neither me nor Betty had come across him during our time in the police, but we did know of him in the way that everyone in the area had heard his name. So we were a clean slate. We were accommodating on price, being new. He probably thought we would follow instructions and give him a whitewash write up that he could use for whatever purpose he had in mind. Then he hadn't done his homework. The police had taught me to take nothing at face value, question everything and trust nobody, especially not anyone making reports to the police. Partridge had come to us, possibly, from a sense of security. He was a rich and successful man, at face value, and he probably had developed a streak of arrogance, as anyone might in that position. He could probably bribe the police if he needed to, but for some reason this wasn't a matter he wanted to take to them. I decided to talk to an old friend for a little background check. After supping up, I walked into the police headquarters.

The main station of the City Police always gave me the shivers. Sometimes public buildings make even the innocent feel guilty, and that's deliberate. Or perhaps it's because none of us are truly innocent of everything all of the time. I made sure the stolen papers were firmly into the bottom of my jacket pocket.

I had been the one to inculcate Inspector Givens into the ways of the force on his first day, a little over ten years ago. We had kept in touch. I hadn't made it beyond sergeant when that unfortunate incident led to the departure of myself and Betty. We'll get into it another time, but without some money from her deceased husband to set up her agency I don't know what I would be doing now.

Givens seated me at his large desk in his corner office, looking a little smug.

"You want to know a little bit about the Lord Line?" he started in. "For a book?"

I smiled. "I see Miss Cool has been very professional in giving the official smokescreen, but it's not necessary. Mr Partridge has retained us. He is my client."

"To write a book?" Givens was smiling broadly.

"To investigate some internal chicanery at the docks. The story as he tells it is that he's been made aware of some under the counter stuff and he has some suspects and wants to get to the bottom of it privately and quietly."

"They always do. Wouldn't it be easier just to come here instead? Save the money? It almost looks like he's up to something, I would say."

I laid out the structure of my thinking to Givens. I held back here and there, edited this and that, didn't mention the burglary or anything that could lose Betty her license or reputation beyond its current low standing in these corridors, and waited. I sipped at a tea someone had thoughtfully brought in. The saucer rattled, as it always does.

"So you want to know if we have any reason to be interested in the Lord Line?" It wasn't a question. Givens stood up and gawped out the window like Betty does when she thinks. It's something about windows. And the police. Was Givens wondering how much to share, or wracking his brains and coming up empty?

"Every large organisation has its ups and downs," he began. "But Lord Line is bigger than most, certainly private companies. It's famous and quite successful, even at this time, so there are envies and jealousies. Employment matters, the odd assault. A fight in the canteen. I would describe this as the usual goings-on.

"Anything like that happen in the last couple of weeks?" I asked, but I got the sense Givens was just on a pause.

"The last time something involved us was a couple of months ago. A fight, perhaps, or more of a scuffle. They wanted to keep it quiet, play it down, and it wasn't anything too serious. We only got involved because the pub landlord's new barmaid phoned it in. Even the landlord said she had over-reacted. We had someone in the area so he strolled around as it was calming down."

"Any names?" I had in mind the lad from the wood shop.

"A Mr Powell and a Mr Southman."

I looked up at that. Not those two? Fighting each other in a bar? "Do you know either of them?" I asked.

"I never met them."

"They're not the sort to hang around fighting in bars, let me put it that way."

"Everyone can have a moment, Ted." He said that with a little more feeling than I liked.

"It would need to be quite something to rile those two up, seriously. It would be like awakening a statue."

"Then it might not be relevant. It's probably about a woman, not about work."

"That's what I thought. Thanks. *Inspector!*"

I arrived at the house just in time for tea with Mrs Pearson. She set it all out beautifully on a silver tray. No butler here, but a maid did the hard bits. Mrs Pearson just brought it into the drawing room of their tidy detached house. A lower league to Partridge and Gelder but still fancy.

"This is quite exciting," she admitted. I took it she meant about the book. Perhaps she was hoping her doilies might make it in somehow. "You're here to interview Mr Pearson? He will be thrilled."

"Not as thrilled as me, Mrs Pearson. It's a real privilege to be allowed into the sanctum of one of the Lord Line's leading lights. I am sure he will have many stories."

"He's been there over years and years, started before the war. Luckily he was too old for any of that so he helped send supplies around Europe. One of our ships was sunk!"

"Perhaps I should be interviewing you, Mrs Pearson. Nobody had mentioned a sinking to me."

"A torpedo! You have to wonder. Many died, but many survived. At the time it was a very tragic thing, but it fades. That was nearly twenty years ago."

"It sounds like Mr Pearson might have been at the Lord Line since school."

She nodded. "That's right. He started in the sheds and worked his way up. Quite a rise, as he will tell you. Quite a rise. Of course it leaves me here at a loose end..."

I made my face look sympathetic. I was sure she could find some gin or cards to keep the maid busy for a turn here and there. Compared to being torpedoed in your bunk it looked a pretty sort of life to me.

There was a rustle in the hall and footsteps. I hoped for Mr Pearson. Last night was catching up on me.

"Hello, Mr Bird! They told me you have been turning over rocks at the office today. I thought we had a meeting for tomorrow?"

I stood up, my saucer rattling once again. "True, Mr Pearson, I do apologise. It's part of my approach. I have been frequenting everyone at home, with them expecting me the next day. I do find the story behind the work really brings colour to the proceedings."

He nodded. "Quite right, clever. I hope Mrs Pearson has been burnishing our brand for you?"

"I thought you might tell him more about that torpedo?" said Mrs Pearson helpfully.

He paused for a moment, as though she had launched one at him. "I'm not sure that's quite the kind of story-"

"Oh it very much is, sir. Readers will be keen to hear how the Lord Line serviced its country in the line of battle and all that stuff. You can count on it."

"Right. Well, of course we were helping move munitions, tanks, anything necessary, for the government. We didn't have much else to push around." He made it sound so magnanimous. On he went, "So we took a few ships over to the continent, and some even across the Atlantic to fetch the Americans when they bothered to get stuck in. We were fed some rubbish about shipping lanes and the Germans torpedoed a boat not far west of Ireland. It sank, but not quickly enough that we couldn't get almost everyone-"

"A hundred men died!" Mrs Pearson cried, and covered her mouth. She retreated from the field of battle. It made me think her sweetheart had been a victim.

"I don't remember the numbers, I'm afraid, Bird. I'm very sure it wasn't a hundred."

"This is quite a story. We can take it up tomorrow, of course. Has anything remarkable happened recently, say in the last year or two?"

He sat down. He made a good show of looking like a thinking man, but my presence and the torpedo had taken his wind. "That's the thing about this, Bird. We're a quiet sort of place. I don't know who would buy a book about an office."

"They're mainly about marketing. Promotional stuff. The war activities are fabulous, they will really bring it to life." I chose the moment to sit next to him. He hadn't noticed I wasn't taking any notes. "Mr Pearson, I am sure a company as large as Lord Line must have a good yarn or two. Anything in the last few weeks?"

He looked startled. "Nothing at all, Bird. Now I'm hungry. Let's resume tomorrow in the office. It was a good idea for you to come here. Well done."

I stood to leave. I expected him to read the rules once again to his errant wife.

# CHAPTER SEVEN

I turned in early with a cocoa. Hot milk works for me, and I can recommend it. My eyelids were drooping before I was in my pyjamas. Next  morning, some rare sunshine. As I was due in Mr Pearson's office at ten o'clock there was no need to drop by and see Betty. I would take it easy. There was bacon in the refrigerator. I started warming up the frying pan and filled the kettle. Pearson was telling me nothing, but his wife had been a revelation. Once you realised the key to my game was small talk with wives who had too few opportunities for chatter, it was much easier. It didn't work everywhere, but these senior executives were as one in spending too many hours in the office and too few at home tending to their domestic concerns. I couldn't understand why Pearson was so touchy about the torpedo attack, which seemed a brilliant advert for the company, far more than any book. It was such a good story that it would ordinarily have become a famous legend associated with the firm. That it was not known about spoke volumes. Sometimes people kept wartime secrets just because they were told to. Admirable though that was, I believed these characters would be shouting it from the rooftops if it helped them in any way.

I believe I had started whistling along with the kettle and had thrown some bacon onto the pan when there was a knock at the door. Expecting Betty or Miss Cool, although I didn't know what either of them would want, I was stunned to see a haunted-looking Inspector Givens on the step. I had no option but to invite him in, unless I was happy to let the bacon burn.

"Good morning, Inspector," I said. "Twice in two days. Follow me to the kitchen where I need to tend some bacon. Fancy a slice?"

"No thanks. It's about your friend at Lord Line."

"Is it? You've found something about Partridge!"

"I would have coffee, if you had some spare," he said, and sat rather awkwardly holding his hat. "I'm afraid to say that Mr Pearson is dead. His wife called us before breakfast."

That rather took the shine off the bacon, which was ready. I turned off the heat and left it in the pan. "Pearson. I've got an appointment with him at ten. Oh God. What happened?"

"We're still figuring out the details."

"He didn't shoot himself?"

"It's highly unlikely his death was accidental, natural or self-inflicted."

"I thought you might say that. And I'm a suspect?"

Givens nodded. "The timing is awful, isn't it, Ted?"

I had to nod. "Really awful. So awful one might thing I had been set up."

"That's my line of thought, too. Lucky and unlucky you popped in yesterday. If you hadn't, it would look bad once things started to point to you. But because you did come in, you're top of the list anyway."

"A lose-lose situation."

"Do you have any thoughts? Some way that we can cross you off quickly?"

"I'm afraid not," I said, although of course I did. I didn't want to share anything with anyone other than Betty. Sooner or later Partridge would be swarming into the office asking hard questions. Either he fitted me up, or someone did so on his behalf, or the whole thing was a terrible coincidence. In real life, coincidences account for events more often than not. I learned that in the army and then again in the police.

"Well I'm here in a personal capacity," said Givens. "Get your story straight and quickly. Next time I'm here it will be for a statement down at the station."

"I'm surprised," I replied, "that this has happened. I thought they got me involved to keep it quiet, not for a convenient fall guy. I'll give you an update tomorrow if I don't see you before that."

I ate the bacon alone, the joy sucked out of the morning. After dressing I took a slow walk to the office to let Betty have the bad news, if she had yet to hear. There are days like that where it would be better if it were foggy. The sunlight on such a morning just mocks you. It's saying yes, people are enjoying my rays and having fun, just not you.

I slowly crept up the stairs to the office, unaware of the time until I saw the clock. It was nine-thirty and I could see the outline of Betty inside her office. Miss Cool stopped me as soon as I arrived.

"Are you all right, Ted?" she asked, a hand on my arm indicating that news of Mr Pearson's demise must have preceded me. "What happened?"

"Not sure. Other than that people leaned on me to talk to Mr Pearson and as soon as I had accomplished that mission he dropped dead within a few hours."

"I never trust a walk-in and I never trusted Mr Partridge," she said. I recognised that our low murmur had come to Betty's attention.

"Morning stranger! You've caused quite a stir. Wander in here."

"Well I haven't done anything of the sort, of course," I said as I sat down. "If anyone is causing a stir it would have to be our client. He set us up to talk to some people and now one of them is dead. I believe that if I had stuck to his plan and talked to him earlier, he would have died earlier. The two things seem closely connected."

"They do. Partridge is going to show up at some stage today. What's his mood likely to be?"

"If he's behind it, he might bluster up some fake anger. If he's not behind it, he might bluster up some genuine anger. Either way, you have to confront him on the fixed price lie now. He can't claim this is some kind of under the counter book cooking. It's not a corporate intrigue any more, it's murder."

"Your thinking is in line with mine," she said. "Luckily he paid up front. Do you think I can risk closing the case and pocketing the money?"

"Yes but it would be a missed opportunity. If we can stay in the game a little longer I am confident we can find a way to capitalise on Partridge's intransigence."

"Would you mind letting me know?"

"The police are involved now, and I've still got a friend or two which could work to our mutual beneficence. I'm likely to be asked to help unravel the murder, not least because I went to them yesterday to chew the cud, quite coincidentally. They're going to want this clearing up pronto. Partridge is going to be on at them, either for the sake of appearances or because he is genuinely angry. Then we will have the press all over it by tonight. This is going to get very hot very fast, just as we made good connections with all of the key players."

"So the smart money is on wait and see?"

I nodded. "Your call of course. The weak way out is to shut the book and tell Partridge what to do with his memoir. But we're not exactly overworked-"

"Thank you Ted, that will be all. Go and rest in your office. I want you here in case Partridge shows up."

I went into my lair to tidy up some more papers.

# CHAPTER EIGHT

"Look, Bird, I need some action on this matter quickly."
It was Partridge, as you guessed, foaming at the mouth in
the outer office. He hadn't bothered to seat himself and
was staring at all three of us in turn, even though it was
my name that came to his lips first. "All you had to do was
talk to the five people and figure out how many of them
were involved, and one of them is in the mortuary!"

When he put it like that, it did sound a little
amateurish on my part. Even Betty, who had agreed that
the five were probably not key suspects, had started to
suggest that I actually pretend to talk to the names on the
list just to calm Partridge down. It wasn't my fault that
Pearson had washed up dead by the river within a day of
my visit. Linking the two events was nothing more than
folly.

"Perhaps the trip to the mortuary should be equated
with guilt?" asked Betty. "The man either panicked and
killed himself or panicked and someone decided he was
too hot and had to be eliminated. Either way, safe to
assume that he was involved. Seems quite neat, actually.
A quick resolution, no need to wait for the courts and all
that."

I couldn't either agree with her or contradict her in front of the client, but I gathered from a certain glance that she was simply pandering to Partridge, most likely in the hope that he would leave without firing us. "Well, you have a point Mrs Abbett, I grant you." He seemed to be taking a breath and engaging his brain. "Okay. I want you to finish off the list Bird, by dusk tonight, and I will return in the morning for a final report. Is that clear?"

We all nodded and looked at our shoes, even Miss Cool, and Partridge made for the exit.

"Just one thing, Mr Partridge," I said. That stopped him. "I want to go on a sea voyage. Get to know the men a little better on ground they find familiar."

"Ground? Ha-ha. You want to spend two months floating around the ocean, Bird?"

"A few hours would be enough. Do you ever take such short trips?"

"All the time. Seaworthiness tests, especially after a big repair job. Be at the docks at dawn tomorrow."

There was an audible collective sigh after his footsteps tapped along the corridor.

"Even the most routine cases turn sour in your hands, Edward," observed Betty, unkindly in my view.

"It seems I should exhaust all avenues suggested by that blasted list before someone else croaks," I admitted. "I'll get on with it, but if he thinks this complicated family matter can be unwound within twenty four hours he's a bigger fool than he seems. I want some quality time with young Mr Southman."

It had been years since I had boarded a boat of any kind. I'd never been good on water and I was expecting a rough couple of hours out in the estuary mouth. It never gets that choppy there. It's still protected from the harsh gales. The mission was a there-and-back test drive to make sure nothing leaked after a repair. There was a larger crew than I expected, monitoring things and keeping an eye out. I supposed a big ship took a lot of manual labour whether it was going to America or Spurn Point.

On the jetty I noticed Jimmy Southman and he recognised me. "Writing up our little adventure for posterity?" he said. Was that a smirk? I was tired and sick of that the stupid memoir story. If the five on the list were somehow up to their necks with Partridge, they would all know the cover story was nonsense from the beginning.

"The man I spoke to after I spoke to you has been murdered," I said, quite coldly. "Watch it."

Left to my own thoughts, I climbed onto the deck and made for the front of the ship, the bow. Steam power was an incredible thing. The smell of coal and hot oil, the steam itself. In a humid climate the steam is ten times worse than it would be, more so on a cold morning. It became a fog that shrouded the deck. Only when we were fully underway would it billow out behind us like a silver ribbon. I relaxed. The law couldn't reach us out here, and another murder was most unlikely. This would be like a holiday were it not for the memories of war, which flooded back at moments like this and almost seemed to be happening again.

The best reason for keeping going with Betty was that it left little time for brooding over the past. If you kept going forward there wasn't time to look behind. As the ship started to move, I did move behind. I walked aft to the stern to watch the city recede. The water chopped up behind a boat this size. It was only at the rear where you could understand the enormous power on display. We were shifting along already, heading for Holland at a slow run. Somewhere among the smokestacks of the old town lay two important answers. What was really going on at the Lord Line? I could see the rectangular office which was more window than wall, and I sensed Partridge watching our departure. And whatever was going on, was Partridge a victim or a criminal? Either one seemed equally likely. Every single event from his original arrival to the dead body could be easily explained away. But if you put them all together in a line, they told a bad story. Partridge was up to something. I just had to talk to enough people to find out. The hard part of this job is not solving mysteries, it is solving them to a deadline. Time is money, but the truth cannot be rushed. A journalist might say that too, but he's not likely to get shot in a dark alley. We're all detectives, aren't we? Trying to unlock the meaning of life. It's hard enough doing it for fun, but it's virtually impossible to make money at it.

"Good morning!" A voice over the roar of the propellers. I turned to find Mr Gelder.

"Good morning, sir," I replied. "Bit of a surprise to see you up here." That was an understatement. I doubted his sea legs.

"I like to get out once in a while." Did he know I was coming? Was he a spy? "I felt it would be safer out here after…"

"You heard about the deceased?"

He nodded sadly. "Terrible shock." He did a good impression of a shocked man.

"How is Mrs P- I mean, you know." Make it look like a slip.

"There are no secrets at Lord Line, are there now?" He looked unruffled. "Any journalist will get to something pretty quickly. There is a lot just under the surface, you know, of such a large and old firm. Everyone's heard of us. Everyone knows someone who once worked for us. I don't have the time, you know. To meet people."

That seemed like his idea of an explanation. It made sense. Old Partridge became boring and old, although he wasn't much older than me and I didn't feel old. He found a younger model and his wife, left out in the cold, jumped onto the next passing vessel.

"You didn't fancy a faster broad?" I said, wondering if he would get my drift.

"Lord no! I'm a simple man, a numbers man. People are a mystery to me, Bird. Mrs Partridge is a very friendly and dependable woman." She certainly was, but I had seen another side. I believed he had not seen it in the decades he must have known her.

I took a turn around the deck, right around the complete circle. At times, I grabbed onto the handrail as the sea rose. I believe its called the taffrail. I felt unwell, and went below decks to prowl. Although I didn't know what I was looking for, I did realise something quickly. As soon as you had watched the town recede out the back of the frothing stern, you were transported to a different world. This world rolled and bucked, but it had a calm silence underneath all the blowing of the whistle, the churning of the propellers and the immense steam from the boilers. Beneath that surface stuff, all was quiet. The men's nerves were settling by the minute. The troubles of home, whether it be money or love, started to weaken their hold on the mind. Even the notion of Mr Pearson's body, washed up on the shore, practically with a note denouncing me as the killer, failed to stir my heart. A little distance worked wonders for the mind, and it wasn't difficult at all to understand why these men loved the sea.

As the ship sailed east, I could no longer make out the riverbanks to our left and right. All around was water, in every direction, and this water had a new characteristic.

It was even less calm. There were proper waves, and the ship began to roll. It was time to turn back. I staggered through the corridors, not sure whether to walk or sit, and decided fresh air would help my stomach. Walking up to the bow I found Southman once again. He was staring out straight ahead. "How's your sea legs, writer?" he asked.

"Wobbly."

"We've turned around. It's always better to watch the horizon when we turn like that. You're doing well for a landlubber. You're past half way." He clumped me on the shoulder and smiled.

"Good," was all I managed to say.

"They're pretty confident of their repairs. Once they write it up she'll be good and ready to sail tomorrow."

"Where?"

"Could be Norway again, could be China. Could be the new world. Even St. Petersburg. I don't care. I prefer it here."

"At sea or in town?"

"In England. I used to sail a little, just helping out now and again. It's overrated. One place is like any other, once you see through the differences."

"Some people like the differences, I suppose," I said. I had to focus on keeping my breakfast inside.

"They're only on the surface, those folks. People are people, wherever you go."

"I agree with you, although many wouldn't. I've seen a few things. Enough to see that you are right. Were you in the war?"

"Of course I was! I won't shirk any responsibility. What's necessary it's what's needed. Now you mention it, that's when I decided I would never leave England again."

He had a point. I had made no final decision, but it was true that I hadn't left since. "You've done a good job on the repair," I said. "What do you know of Charlie Wilson?"

"He's friendly enough. I don't see him much in the sheds. I see him in the pub sometimes. He's often with the same guy, or at least in the same pubs at the same time. A Mr Powell, I believe."

Powell was the first man on Partridge's list. He had been too busy to see me. "Anything remarkable about Powell or Wilson?"

"No, just that I see them together more often than one would expect. They operate at opposite ends of the pecking order, if you see what I mean. You wouldn't catch me in the same room as Partridge or Gelder more than once every two years."

I walked off for a final circuit of the deck before the town would emerge at the bow. When I returned to the bow, he was gone. I could see the smoke stacks of the docks, the tower of the minster church, and other big ships being loaded and offloaded. It was a busy place, growing fast. I wasn't pulled to the far corners of the world by curiosity any longer, and I didn't much care for the silence of the sea. Men like Jimmy Southman could not help but fill the void with idle chatter. I was drawn to the hustle and bustle, the low lives and the double dealing. That was an honest kind of life, it seemed to me. People said what they thought and fought each other when they disagreed. Fine talking men like Partridge and Gelder were shallow. They hid behind accountants and lawyers and private investigators, believing they held all the cards. But their tricks were logical tricks. Put them in a bar against a man armed with a snooker cue and they melted like snowmen. Put them on the wrong side of a loaded gun and they would, quite honestly, lose the number of their mess.

I had managed to walk onto dry land, taking great gulps of air against a topsy turvy stomach, when I heard a shout. There was some kind of commotion going on, and I became aware that Mr Gelder could not be found.

# CHAPTER NINE

"Thanks for coming out," said Jimmy Southman, cradling his beer at the Old Town pub.

"Any information can be useful," I replied. I watched Ethel lurking in the background over the top of my glass as I raised it. She was entertaining a group of gentlemen with one of her stories, but she caught my eye.

"There's something going on, even overlooking the corpse and the missing Mr Gelder," Southman stated. "I don't mean some book writing rubbish, I mean something real and... sinister."

I replaced my glass on the table and indicated that he should continue with that thought. I always thought he was the most likely one of the five to actually know something. It's always the boots on the ground who know what's really happening. "What's your theory?"

"It's not a theory. It's a few bits and pieces. Things said, things not said."

"You think someone's on the fiddle?" I suggested. I was deliberately leading him. I had the feeling it was more complicated than that.

"Someone's always fiddling someone. It's a big, famous company. Long heritage. Everyone's fiddling. A timesheet here, a friend clocking off for you. Then at the top there's big fiddles but the police and them always overlook the big stuff. They only get excited when it's our lot doing the fiddling."

"Come, come, Mr Southman. I don't need a lesson in the ways of the world." I tried to sound kind but I had to make him talk before Ethel got near.

"This is top level stuff. Not just criminality. Something... I don't know what word to use. Big. I mean beyond the shipping line. Much beyond."

I had a think about that. Bigger than criminal. Well, one criminal offence on the list was murder. There wasn't much in the world considered bigger than murder. In the eyes of the law... "You mean treason!" I blurted out.

That knocked Southman for six. He grabbed at his beer, almost knocked it over, and flicked his eyes around the room. "Quiet, Mr Bird. That's not the word I would use, but that's what I mean. It involves a... foreign power."

"Why have you come to this answer?"

"Like I said, it's nothing too solid. But there are certain trips we do, to particular places, that attract attention. Different faces go on those ships. Mysterious faces. Strange things happen at sea all the time, but if you look at certain trips, to particular places, things... go wrong. More often than you would expect."

"What sort of places?"

"St. Petersburg. The Baltic generally, actually."

And over came Ethel. Was she sauntering or staggering? Either way, she took Southman's attention for a few minutes during which I received my composure. I don't think even Partridge had expected anything like this. In that instant, I began to think Partridge too had genuine suspicions, and that his decision to involved me was entirely above board. Could it be that Partridge was a victim too? The name of the firm he had given his working life to was at risk from chisellers unknown and now possibly even the USSR itself. It seemed incredible to me, but not so incredible that I wouldn't give it careful thought. Ports are international places. They link continents by well-established trading routes. Once you start sailing to somewhere else, no matter how far away it was, you were connected. The boats allowed the traffic of people and had served spies well in the war. Could they still be enabling the Communists to spy on the folk of Kingstown? No. But Kingstown is only a day's travel from London. I shuddered.

"Southman. Do you believe that spying stuff yourself, having seen and heard what you have?"

He gave that some thought. "Yes I do. It might sound strange but it's an explanation for everything that has happened."

"And Gelder?"

"A mystery to me."

Partridge was in the office before me and Betty the following morning, which gave me some intimate time to apply thumbscrews.

"Mr Partridge. Good day to you, sir. The very man. Gelder turned up yet?"

"I'm afraid not. This is a very bad business."

I nodded. "I have to level with you, sir. Time to talk turkey."

It was his turn to nod. He seated himself in my less commodious office and I stood where the window would have been if we were in Betty's. I tried to look official and determined. "Ok, Mr Bird. Go ahead."

"I had a hankering that you were trying to set me up for the murder of Pearson. Not surprising when you add in the fact that I asked for permission to have a sail around the estuary and then Gelder disappears, presumed drowned at sea."

"I'm not offended. It seems logical to me."

"So you're not going to all this trouble just to get rid of a couple of undesirables who haven't been naughty enough to get themselves sacked?"

He shook his head. "It's a very plausible explanation, but it's not true. I'm as mystified as you are."

"So you don't know anything about St. Petersburg?"

He raised an eyebrow, and let it settle. He shook his head. "This is a very bad business. I had suspicions about some of my staff, and they have been proved to be wide of the mark. Whatever is going on is more serious than I suspected. I have the police and newspapermen crawling all over the docks. Our reputation is in ruins."

"A less reasonable client might blame me for not investigating fast en0ugh. I have something for you." I pulled out the documents we had stolen and set them alongside the forgeries. "I have proof that someone has been faking up paperwork to hide their stealing. It's more like smuggling when you consider the amounts involved. This is highly organised criminal activity."

Mr Partridge looked carefully at the documents, comparing one with the other repeatedly. "The numbers are different and nothing else, not the dates, or the invoice numbers, or the lading codes. The signatures match. You don't think the person who signed these is involved, I take it?"

I shook my head. "Too obvious. These have been duplicated, not signed twice, and then the numbers doctored. One for management and the accountants, customs and officialdom. And then the real ones, hidden in the bottom drawer. The fakes understate every single number by quite a margin. They must have had transport to take this quantity of stuff away from the docks. This is a gang, Mr Partridge. I would suggest your security people are involved, at least to the extent of turning a blind eye."

"This is good work. I won't ask how you came by these files. A couple of days ago I would have walked away thinking I had the answers I needed. You've done good work Mr Bird. But today..."

"Yes, things have certainly turned against us. There's no question of us proceeding on the old arrangement, I'm sorry to say."

He understood what I meant. "When Mrs Abbett arrives I will retain you to get to the bottom of this new mystery."

"I'm afraid that our rate..." I trailed off. He nodded again. "And I must ask you one more thing before I leave you with Betty. Don't investigate the smuggling yet. I have given you the information you need to catch the gang. But there is a possibility - I would say a likelihood - that the gang are wrapped up in Pearson, Gelder and whatever else is going on. It's not certain, but I don't want to blow the big case by rounding up the small-timers."

"I see. I will wait. Are these the original documents? Well, ha, I mean, do you require copies for your use?"

"Miss Cool already xeroxed them." I could see the silhouette of Betty through the glass, and I decided to slip out the side door and down the fire escape. She would find it easier than she might have expected to negotiate more favourable terms with Mr Partridge for our continued benefit.

I was suddenly spoilt for choice on leads. I had Gelder to find, I had a Russian angle, there was still the Pearson murder, Michael Powell, and I had resolved to believe

Mr Partridge. I could not extend the same courtesy to his new lady friend or, indeed, his legal wife. In helping Mr Partridge to understand the scale of the smuggling operation at Lord Line, we had only multiplied the mysteries. One door closes and another opens. I decided that a weak beer and a chat with Ethel was just the thing.

She saw me straight away and came over, full of energy. "Mr Southman was quite the dish," she stated loudly. "I've been thinking..."

"So have I. What do you think about his tale?"

"You think it's a tale as well?"

"That's not what I meant, but go on."

She told me that she had remained until closing time in the bar with him last night, and he had walked her home. She had the distinct impression that he was making up stories. Although I hadn't had full time to look back on his claims, she had a point. "The Russian story was so far-fetched I thought it had to be true," I said, somewhat lamely. "You don't believe a word of it?"

She shook her head. "I do not. But it might not be as simple as making the whole thing up. Good liars only change some bits to protect the guilty, and stick to the facts where they can."

"That had occurred to me too, after ten years of police work and a war spent in the front line, as it goes."

She looked hurt and I decided that another drink would calm her down. This was the part I didn't like. You remember how much I like the first few days on a new case? Everything is easy and gentle and fun. Well this is the part where there are so many corridors it's like a maze. You can't believe a word anyone says at all, which made it all the more reassuring to be able to believe Partridge, at least for now. The only thing worse than this would be to have our client lying through his teeth on top of everything.

"What would you do next, Ethel?"

"I would talk to Lana Partridge again. Her real name is Lana Turner, if you can believe it."

"That's really the name she goes by?"

"It's very clever. If it's true, it's true and she can't use any other name, now can she? But if it's made up then it's so blatant that people will assume it's *not* made up."

"You really can't remember anything else about her?"

Ethel shook her head. "Just that she's not to be trusted, believed or relied upon for anything up to and including the weather report."

"And what do you think about the man who went missing at sea?"

"He's either drowned or he's involved."

"Or both," I said. I couldn't believe Gelder getting involved in anything but then, he was one of the men on the list. If we now thought Partridge was honest it meant Partridge had genuine suspicions about Gelder. "I need a holiday," I said.

"Let's go!"

"Maybe tomorrow. I'm going out to Anlaby for a cocktail lunch. Thanks, Ethel. Here's something for another drink."

# CHAPTER TEN

It should be clear that I was heading for the hall at a time I knew Mr Partridge would be absent. If I had managed to persuade myself that he was on the level, the same could not be said for his new girlfriend. Lana Turner had the name, the background and the carriage of a girl on the make, and I didn't want to make the same mistake with her as with Partridge. Just because he was honest didn't make her so. But it didn't make her bent either. I had to find out. Why was she so accommodating on my first visit? Her omission from Mr Partridge's list was telling.

This time I walked the length of the drive. Taking my time enhanced the grandeur. A curving, meandering private drive is designed to show off and intimidate. Partridge might not have built the place but he bought it. This was the fitting approach to the home of the man at the helm of Lord Line. It might not be too long before he himself became a Lord or a Sir, as long as I did my job. The fog that was hanging over his career and livelihood had gotten thicker since I turned up. This fact was wearing away at me, perhaps more so than Partridge. He could retire tomorrow. I couldn't even afford tomorrow's rent.

The lodgekeeper let me through without fuss, and I stepped onto the gravel drive. A slate sky began generating its customary rain as I approached the house. Lana Turner seemed an odder character the more I heard about her. Could it be as simple as a girl on the make? By the evidence of this house she had achieved her goal. But Ethel seemed close to her, protective. I trusted Ethel's judgement. She was as shrewd an interrogator as anyone I met during my years on the force. She had helped Betty and I during the case that led to the abrupt changes last year, and she knew everyone in those old town bars. Knowing those people, mainly men, gave her connections across the city. Ethel could connect you to just about anyone via her friends of friends.

It was the housekeeper who opened the door, and she was in at least two minds until I set her straight. I wasn't walking back to the lodge so she might as well announce my arrival. She nodded and showed me back into the drawing room.

"Mr Bird! Such a thrill! You must have enjoyed our little evening?"

I nodded. "I come on a personal matter, Mrs Turner." I had always wondered how to address the woman. Ethel hadn't mentioned a former husband, but I tried out the Mrs on a whim. It had an effect, but not much of one. Her eyes fluttered a little and she forced a smile.

"Please, take a seat."

"Your- Mr Partridge. He's in a fix, honestly. There's poor Mr Pearson, and now Gelder is missing."

She seated herself next to me, closer than normal. She nodded gravely. "It's very sad. I'm worried about all the boys."

"Does Mr Partridge seem all right to you? Anything change in the last few weeks?"

She snorted. "He works long hours and when he's at home he's preoccupied. It's always been that way."

"Always since you moved in? When would that have been?"

She hesitated. "Six months, perhaps."

"I thought perhaps it was more recently."

"I don't know how or why, Mr Bird, but I wouldn't have thought I would have lasted two weeks. I know what I was getting into, you know. I'm not as naive as I look."

"I don't think you look naive, Mrs Turner." She didn't. She looked worldly wise to me. Whatever she was looking for, she had certainly made it financially. All she needed now was a marriage certificate. "Pardon me, Mrs Turner, but these are pressing times. Has Mr Partridge formally divorced as yet?"

That did it. She shot out of that chair like a bullet. She stood by the window and put a hand to her mouth. I waited, still seated. I waited some more.

"I don't think he wants to marry me, Mr Bird. I think he regrets our little scenario here and I think he's trying to figure out a way to get Mrs Partridge back here."

I swallowed. "I thought something like it myself. It doesn't make the disappearance of Mr Gelder look good, does it?"

She looked at her shoes. She just shook her head. "Mr Bird?" She looked up at me then, her eyes wet with something deep. I wasn't going to press it now. "Mr Bird. Let's be clear on something. Mr Partridge is in genuine need of help. He needs you to unravel whatever is going on at the docks. His personal life is a mess. If we cared what the neighbours said we would never step out of the grounds. But he did not kill Mr Pearson and whatever happened to that old fool Gelder is nothing to do with Mr Partridge. Please listen to that and remember it."

"I believe you, Mrs Turner. I will do what I can."

I left her then. She never did correct the Mrs. I did the one thing there was to do. I walked back to the lodge and carried on walking until I arrived at Mr Gelder's house. There's something about walking. It gives you time to reflect. The motion calms the nerves. Mrs Turner's emotions had their effect on me, and no doubt. She had so much bottled up emotion she must be turning crazy in that big house all on her own, after the tough life she had led until meeting Mr Partridge. But the approach needed for Mrs Partridge would be altogether more subtle. Her new squeeze was missing, presumed drowned at sea, and she could hardly imagine the unrest at Partridge Towers. Her reaction to Mr Gelder's disappearance would tell me a lot, but I had to be alert and ready to listen more than talk. Funny thing about the police and investigators is they think the job is all about talking and cracking wise. It's not. That's the smoke screen that helps you to listen. They think you're some wise guy on the take and then they spill their guts and you just mop it up and throw them over to the law. It worked on men like a charm, but their wives, well. They're cannier animals. I understand Betty, and I understand Ethel. And I can't promise that I understand a single other one of them. I only understand those two because they're straight up and down on the level without guile. Or if they use guile it's so guileful that I can't register it.

"Good afternoon, Mrs Partridge. I find that I have missed my lunch. Would you care for a bite in the village?" She went off to find a coat. She didn't look distressed but she wasn't skipping around either.

"Terrible business about Alfred, isn't it?" I said as we walked out of the gate.

"Have you heard anything?" she asked me. "They're not saying much and either they don't know or won't say."

"Nobody knows anything. I was on the ship when he disappeared and I didn't notice anything at all. No attitude or whispers. He just vanished. Was he under any kind of pressure?"

"Of course he was! They all are. Pearson was a terrible shock. But things have been going wrong for a long time now, a couple of years. That's why you were brought in. Whatever they know they're not telling me and if I had to guess I would say they didn't know anything. Whatever is going on is at some superior level, somehow. It's outside the Lord Line because Alfred and my husband don't know the first thing about it."

"And you believe them?" She ordered the Welsh rarebit again. A creature of habit.

She nodded. "I do as it happens."

"What will you do, I mean, if..." Sometimes it's better to trail off.

"Well the whole thing is that we're not married, as you know. I have no clue what's in his will and I doubt he even changed it. People never do, especially those with the most to share out. I think you know that I'm still Mrs Partridge."

I just nodded. "Have you heard from Lana since, Mr Gelder... I thought she might send flowers or something."

"You won't believe it but she marched right up to the door with flowers herself. She had tears in her eyes, I swear it. We had some tea and spoke about Mr Gelder and she even spoke about Mr Partridge. You won't believe it."

"Won't believe what?"

"Well, believe it or not we have ways of communicating that go beyond speech." I smiled at that. "And I'm damned if she isn't looking for a way out of that house. Call it wishful thinking but I think she has come around to my view on the man."

"Wishful thinking, Mrs Partridge? Perhaps you have some regrets too?"

She hesitated. "You're a sharp customer, Mr Bird, I'll give you that. All I am saying is that she's bored witless up in that house on her own, just like I was. So guess what? I'm taking a leaf out of your book."

That stopped me. I put down my fork and looked her in the eye. "What do you mean?" I whispered.

"Me and Lana are going into town tomorrow to make a night of it. Kick off our shoes for a couple of hours."

"I have to advise against it." I had to keep Lana and Ethel apart, especially with Mrs Partridge on the scene.

"Quite impossible. I told her you would pick us up at seven and no excuses. You're going to be our chaperone, to make sure those young bucks don't trouble the eye-catching young lady. And we might need you to help her back into the cab at the end of the night."

There isn't too much to say about the evening. We all turned up together in a cab, being careful to choose a pub as far away from Ethel's regular haunts as possible. We all had a few drinks, and the girls loosened up. My feeling was that they had found common cause against the same man, it was quite strange at first.

Sure enough, though, Ethel's lure had bewitched Mrs Partridge. "Let's go an meet your friend Ethel," she said. "She knows how to have fun."

There was no flicker of recognition on Lana's face, and I had been wondering whether we should try to stage a coincidence for half an hour. I don't know why I wanted to keep the two women apart other than caution. If they got talking about the old times, although it could lead to some new information, it could just as easily lead to my unmasking as more than Mr Partridge's biographer. Ethel would know what not to say, but you never knew. With Eileen Partridge pestering me, and my own thoughts equally split, eventually Lana caved in. "I knew an Ethel once, in these pubs," she said. And off we went.

It made the evening. Lana recognised Ethel immediately across the smoky bar and they got catching up on the last couple of decades, including a war and whatever else could happen in half a lifetime. It was easy to see why Mr Partridge had fallen for her, and I settled in next to his wife. She was relaxing to talk to, and I wondered again at how the two men in her life had never even met the real Eileen Partridge. Life can be funny like that. Without dragging out the old cliché file, life is endlessly varied and surprising.

# CHAPTER ELEVEN

I had the police on my doorstep the next morning. They were still faffing around over the Pearson murder, accident, or other ill-tide.

"It's true, we're stuck on Pearson. But this is about Gelder. Something washed up."

"What, a hand?" I wasn't in the mood.

"Some clothing."

"That doesn't mean a thing. Have you ever been on a boat?"

I showed the officer into the kitchen once again, and half-thought about repeating the routine with the bacon for nostalgia. He sat down heavily. "No, I haven't. There are people inspecting that boat and they didn't find Mr Gelder. Perhaps that's not surprising, but there's no trace of him anywhere else."

"We didn't dock anywhere. We were gone a few hours and we didn't stop."

"I don't know whether to ask for help or to arrest you."

"I won't be much help in a cell at the station. If I'm out on my own recognisance I might dig something up. I had a very interesting evening myself."

He looked up.

"I want to take a close look at Partridge's girlfriend. She styles herself Lana Turner and nobody knows if she's winding you up. But she's not happy, and she's on the make."

"I hardly think she's murdered two slightly overweight middle-aged men."

"There's more than one way to kill a man."

"Poison?"

"Possibly. I was thinking more about hiring someone else to do the difficult jobs. And what have you heard about a Russian link to the Lord Line?"

The officer stood up sharply. "This all sounds like nonsense to me. A hit man?"

"Just one of the many open avenues I am proceeding along. Do you have anything you can share that might help?"

There was always something. It was just a case of how honest he was, or dishonest, and how much he really though I had to do with all the bad luck for Partridge and family.

"Gelder has previous," he said, and left, just like that.

If that was true, Ethel would know something about it. But so would Partridge himself, unless... unless it was so long ago, back in his ancient youth. In which case nobody but he would know. Unless. Surely a man his age had been married? I dismissed all notion of bacon and made a beeline to the records office. If he had been married, I needed to speak to his wife urgently. There was no time to ask Miss Cool to do it.

I found Mr Gelder eating toast with some old camp coffee stuff that he said he preferred to the newer instant granules. He was smoking and reading the Daily Telegraph. His former wife, whom I quickly established was in fact still married to him, even had some real butter and she applied it to the toast for me. The Telegraph, its crossword half-complete, lay in front of him. He sucked on the arm of his spectacles.

"If you don't tell anybody where I am, I'll answer your questions," he had said, which was all I wanted. I'm not a journalist and I'm no longer with the police. Private affairs are private. He began to talk. "I had to do something. Old Pearson was just the first. I figured I would be next if I just waited around. I jumped off the front of the ship, to the side, so that the ship didn't cut my head off in the water. I swam to the shore and waited for my dear wife to collect me. She had towels and a change of clothes, and I've been here since."

"The police haven't been?"

He shook his head. Not yet. We have an early warning system which involves me hiding in a cupboard if they show up.

"Did you do that today?" He nodded. Once he realised I wasn't going away he showed his face. "You really think you're in danger? You must know the rig they've got going on. Are you part of that?"

He shook his head sadly. "If I had known how tight things would get I would have got into it. I deserve compensation for my innocence. Perhaps you feel that sometimes?"

"Given that the police think I offed Pearson, yes I do. Sometimes the fees we charge are so low we might as well do it for fun."

"Well I don't even get a fee. I see things, I hear things, I pretend not to. But when you get to a certain level, even things you don't really know about become your problem. A scandal would rock the boat. It's a big enough town but a company the size of the Lord Line cannot afford a scandal."

"So what's really going on?"

He told me what he knew, and it quickly emerged that he had about half the story. No mention of any Russians. Or he was lying. Or the Russian thing was just gossip. He mentioned something about the smuggling and the fake paperwork, and joined some dots that didn't hang together. He had a theory that Pearson was causing trouble and so they did away with him. But Pearson was found on the shore. Perhaps he had tried to fake his own death like Gelder? "I believe he was murdered. Are the post mortem results in yet?"

I shook my head. "They're slow. You haven't heard about Russians? Perhaps they are the destination for the smuggled stuff? Wouldn't it be easier to hide the stuff at the far end than in the nose of the security guards at the docks here in town?"

Gelder thought about that. "Perhaps. But then you can only smuggle from that one end, on a small fraction of the ships. If you cart the stuff away from this end, you can skim a smaller amount from every single load, if you wanted to."

That really made sense. "So what are you going to do now? How long will you hide?"

"Permanently. We're leaving town as quickly as possible. I've had enough of that place and those people. We're off."

"You won't claim any life insurance?" That would make things difficult for me if he did something like that.

"No. We're going as we arrived in this world, with innocence. I will get a job in the new place, which I won't tell you, using some family connections. Nobody will really miss me and with luck that awful Mrs Partridge will return to her husband."

None of them had seen the real Mrs Partridge, I thought to myself as I pulled the squeaky gate shut behind me. I whistled as I walked along the pavement, and the sun showed its face from behind a cloud.

As I had to walk for a while, it was a chance to review the case so far. Clearly I would keep Mr Gelder's secret exactly as long as I needed to, and long enough for him to leave town. He was the only sensible one of the lot of them. Nobody ever regretted selling early, or leaving the table before midnight. Cut your losses was a strategy I never followed and always regretted ignoring. Gelder was sensible, and he had even seen fit to return to his wife. I wondered how many men like he and Partridge left their wives for younger models, only to be disappointed that the newness soon wore off. At a certain age, I could only too easily imagine, familiarity and home comforts became the most attractive proposition. Ethel had warned me about the complexities of pandering to men, men who didn't know what or who they wanted, who they were or where they were going. They loved her as long as it took them to find those things out, which was never longer than half a night, and they left happy and back on the right track. Ethel was the most sensible person he knew, after Betty Abbett. And Miss Iris M. Cool, of course. The men were always fools without their women. Except for Gelder.

So with Pearson dead and Gelder gone, the temperature rose as the list of suspects shortened. If Partridge was playing a straight bat then... the name Southman came into my head, unbidden. Southman. Now that was a name. Not a name like Lana Turner, but a name nonetheless. It was a name that sounded unusual, and not in a credible way. Southman, in the north. A man from the south, just visiting our northern foggy shores. Southman.

The next morning, having adjusted to the new facts, I returned to the office. Partridge honest, Pearson dead, Gelder removed by his own hand. Southman still in the frame for something. But Lana Turner and Mrs Partridge were far from excluded. Why was it that male clients always looked for male suspects? The women of Anlaby knew more than the men would have dreamed and, because the women talked to each other, they had more information to join together. The men were secretive, they competed against each other and vied for authority. They only collaborated just until one of them got bigger ideas and threw the other one in front of the trolleybus. The women, without aspirations along the same lines, were forced to share. Perhaps some of them reported back to their husbands, but not all.

"If I told you, Miss Cool, that both Pearson, being dead, and Gelder, being missing, were innocent and that Partridge was telling the straight truth, what would you say?"

"Partridge could be telling the truth and still killed Pearson," she replied quickly. "What do you make of the wives?"

"That is the question, isn't it?"

Betty arrived looking tired, her spark faded. "Any news, Ted?"

"Yes, plenty. But we're still at the stage where the more we know, the more confused we get."

"That's the part I hate," she replied. "If only there was some way to jump through this bit. Would it help to run anything past me?"

We settled in her room with tea and biscuits. Neither of us needed the coffee this morning. I hadn't slept well after my return from Mr Gelder's bolthole. Betty and me talked the facts over, tried a few what-ifs and for-instances, and shot ideas back and forth, and we realised some obvious things. It's surprising how often you miss the obvious when you get stuck into the details of a case. We had missed the fifth man, who was actually the first man on Partridge's list. Michael Powell. We had spoken to Pearson, Gelder, Southman and Charles Wilson and totally missed Powell. He had pretended to be busy when I called. I felt at the time that with the stolen paperwork proving the theft, the case had been drawing to an end. We had earned our fixed price and were preparing to close things out when Pearson disappeared. I beckoned Miss Cool into my office and we reviewed all five names up on the blackboard I kept in there for this kind of thing. We put all the names up there, analysed the paper they were written on, and brought out not just the files we shared with Partridge but the whole stack. Betty joined us with rolls from the bakery and we forensically went through everything we knew, including my encounter with Gelder the previous afternoon, which won praise from Betty.

After that session the three of us had a number of new leads, and I sauntered out of there eager and keen to pursue them. It's amazing how often you overlook things in this game, and just one of those tiny fragments is needed to solve the whole thing. Or at least, to set you on that one true path to enlightenment.

# CHAPTER TWELVE

The first thing to mention about the new leads is that word travels fast. It was clear that finding the last man on Mr Partridge's list would not be as easy as the other four. With Gelder presumed dead by all but me, and Pearson very dead, Powell had disappeared. They hadn't seen him at Lord Line since Gelder's escape routine and I didn't blame him. He wasn't married, which made my back channels investigation route a dead-end. Ethel hadn't heard of him which all got me thinking he was probably a Quaker or Methodist and indeed the Wesleyans were very helpful. Mr Powell had toddled off on a retreat due to great stresses upon his person. They folded pretty quickly and pointed me to a monastery on the northern moors. Not feeling up to such a journey on my own I debated the pros and cons of Ethel over Miss Cool and decided that Miss Cool had earned the right to close out our investigation. Whether she would be released by Betty was a trickier angle to cover.

"Who will answer the phones?" was the first question, and it hung in the air like bacon grease for a few seconds. I waited and waited, and never did answer that question. "Is it the only way?"

"It's the safe way. People are going missing and washing up dead and now Powell's escaped our clutches. You might have reminded me about him sooner, but really it's nobody's fault. He's been avoiding me. We didn't buy Partridge's story from the off and everyone on the list proved so fruitful..."

"You have two days. That's one night. A twin room. I'm not paying for two rooms to save anyone's blushes. Tell them you're married but you've got a bad back and can't conceive a double bed. Take the minimum needed for expenses and report every four hours. If you can't get to a phone send a telegram, anything."

An hour later we were on the train to Whitby. Miss Cool made one comment about needing more time to pack, but this was more than offset by two days' all expenses paid in Whitby, even if it was autumn and we were likely to be kept awake by the dreaded fog horns all night. An away day really helped an investigation sometimes. No need to look after life's essentials such as cooking and cleaning and finding clean clothes, and no distractions from other matters in life, or suspects encroaching, or even the police waking me up with terrible news. A road trip was self-fulfillingly exciting, wherever the destination.

"You don't think they will let us just stroll into a monastery?" asked Miss Cool, even before we were north of Beverley.

"No we need to come up with a story. The memoir thing won't work on them. I think some form of religious angle might help. Furthering the cause of God. They won't be able to refuse."

"Do I look religious to you?"

Of course, she knew that she didn't. It wasn't the cherry lips or the modern blouse or any single thing on its own, but Miss Cool was dressed for the office, for a front of house role, and she took modern fashions as seriously as any Methodist believed in the holy father. She would need boring off a few notches on the glamour dial, but otherwise she would be fine. "I'll think of something," I said. "I think we just need to lose all the make-up. And we'll find you an overcoat or a sack or something."

To her credit, she smiled, but only thinly.

There was something magical about a steam locomotive. The more so given that it's end was in sight. Diesel and electric were being tried out and both made sense. Lots of things make sense without being fun. Efficiency is usually dull. Nobody would choose a motor car over a trap and four horses, unless they were going more than five miles of course. No doubt in London, in those underground tunnels, steam and coal were an appalling thought. But out here, in the wilds of the north east, there seemed little problem. We would be at Whitby by lunch time, and who could want to go faster than that?

The landlady at the guesthouse, Mrs Currie, wasn't buying the married couple routine.

"It's lucky I know Mrs Abbett from her many holidays here..."

I caught Miss Cool's eye and I'm afraid to say we laughed. "We're not married, which I think is a relief to all of us," I said. "We're here on *professional* matters, as you can probably understand if you know Mrs Abbett."

The woman's mouth fell open. "A case?!"

Miss Cool nodded gravely and with a straight face. She looked at her shoes, and I decided she would need some different ones for the Methodist retreat. "Mrs Currie, what shoe size are you?" I asked, and the blessed lady cottoned on immediately.

She returned with a pair of the plainest old shoes you ever saw. "I've had a think," she said, "and in view of the businesslike nature of your stay here, and it being of only one night, I do have a spare room, free of any financial burden, on the grounds that such arrangement would be very clearly laid out before Mrs Abbett on your return..."

I said yes even faster than Miss Cool. I had no wish for her to become privy to my nocturnal routines which, some say, include the most aggressive snoring and mad ramblings long into the early hours. I even carried Miss Cool's unfeasibly heavy case up to the third floor landing. Even better, I was down on the first floor, so any audible embarrassment couldn't possibly be connected by her ears to my snorting mouth. "I'll see you downstairs in one hour. And remember. No make-up, put these awful shoes on, and if you don't have something loose, we'll fetch you one of Mrs Currie's overcoats."

"I understand, sir. Anything in the line of duty."

Colour drew to her cheeks when she said that, and she closed the door rather abruptly.

Mrs Currie did provide Miss Cool with a coat and we walked up the 199 steps to the retreat, which was up on the headland close to the famous Abbey. I didn't recall it at the time but the Abbey is mentioned in the novel Dracula as being the site where Dracula himself, in the form of a dog, arrives in England by ship, a ship that crashes and breaks on these very same wild shores. The choice of retreat could hardly have been more appropriate.

"You remember the story?" I checked with Miss Cool.

"I'm looking to join up and you, my uncle, are driving me around and keeping me out of trouble for the duration. We heard about the retreat as we're local folks and thought it would be worth our time to show up. Could I possibly sit in one of the sessions..."

"And while you're in there taking notes, he's bound to notice you. I just know it. And clamp onto him like an old barnacle while I submit our first report to Betty."

The scene was set. If Powell knew anything, I knew that Miss Cool would find it out quicker than I. While she was inside, I popped down the steps again to the post office, sent a vague but positive telegram, and walked around the harbour. We knew that the afternoon session would end by four o'clock so I had two hours to reflect on the case so far. I found these thoughts so much easier to arrange in new surroundings. The clearing effect of a change of scenery is powerful, and I thought as I watched two men hauling lobster crates onto the wall for cleaning. As it would be dark by four, their day was almost done and they just had to prepare the boat for a dawn return to the sea.

I found myself pacing, anxious at what Miss Cool might find out. Although we were only interested in Powell for the sake of completeness, of covering all of Mr Partridge's suggestions, I did find his disappearance on some retreat convenient. The logical assumption was that he had panicked after Pearson washed up and found the simplest ruse he could to escape town. Much like Gelder but with less drama. No doubt Gelder would rather have come on a retreat for a few days than taking a bath in the choppy river and risking death beneath one of his own ships. They were a funny lot at Lord Line.

Eventually I returned to the kipper smoker's hut at the bottom of the 199 steps and began to climb. Unbelievably, I ran into Miss Cool and a man I presumed to be Mr Powell halfway up. They were seated on the bench there and deep in conversation. Experience taught me to keep on walking past, pretending I didn't recognise anyone. I stole a glance at Miss Cool at the last second and reassured myself that she was in control of whatever situation was occurring. I carried on to the top of the steps. When I turned around, they had left the bench, and I ran back down two or three at a time so that I could get close enough to act if anything went wrong. I had not thought that Miss Cool might be in danger, and I did not believe that she was, but this assignation was not part of our plan. She must have hit it off with Powell so well that he suggested either tea or a cocktail in the town, and she felt compelled to accept. She must have realised they would cross my path as they made their way down into the town, this being the only direct route down the steep hillside. I still felt annoyed, and had to duck in and out of doorways as they progressed along the cobbled streets. They walked past several pubs and I realised they were heading to a fish and chip place for an early dinner. So not only would I be standing out in the cold as darkness fell, I would be surreptitiously watching them stuffing their faces. I began rehearsing a complaint for when Miss Cool eventually managed to give Powell the slip.

After a cold wind blew in, and with the sun completely gone, Mr Powell finally emerged from the fish restaurant and he was on his own. Once I was sure he wasn't just stretching his legs, I plunged in to find Miss Cool and order some food of my own in a state of high irritation.

"Good evening, Ted," she said in greeting, and she had such a wide smile on her face that I allowed my irritation to cool. I forcibly gained the attention of a waitress and ordered the largest plate of whatever they wanted to cook. It was usually haddock in these parts.

"You deviated from the plan, Miss Cool. A field operative must do so from time to time, and sometimes these risks pay off. Let's hear what Powell's been thinking about."

"For a God-fearing man he spent a lot of time trying to get into my knickers," she replied. I registered no surprise so she continued. "He wasn't running or hiding from anything at Lord Line," she said. "I'm quite certain. He is missing the office, being a single man, but he comes up here every month or two regularly. He knew about Pearson but that wasn't the reason for him coming up here."

"So what was it?"

"He admitted he was in shipping and freight. I didn't mention Partridge or Lord Line or anything close to it. He spoke of a delivery he had to be on hand for. I got the distinct impression that some load is arriving by rail or road, and being offloaded here at the docks."

"I thought they only handled fish here."

"Apparently this is not fish."

"When is it happening?"

"Either tomorrow night or the night after. He said he was going home on Friday and the precise details depended on the tides and whatnot."

I groaned inwardly. This meant another night or two up here with nothing to do during the days, Miss Cool to babysit and Betty going on about expenses. Trouble was, I couldn't send Miss Cool home now that she was the one with the contact.

"Cheer up! It'll be fun," she said. "We can be tourists in the day time."

"How can you be sure? We need to shadow this man every hour of the day and night."

"He attends the retreat during the days. He's very much a night operator."

"That won't be enough for Betty. It's not enough for me. I think this is our one chance to understand what's been going on at Lord Line."

She thought about that.

"How do you know he isn't doing the smuggling right now?" I asked.

"I can't be one hundred percent certain, but I know that he isn't."

I had to weigh up Miss Cool's intuition and first-hand knowledge of the man with the possibility that she had been utterly deceived.

"Anyway," she continued, "it won't be a problem if I'm wrong."

"Why not?"

"He's staying on the second floor, just above your head and beneath mine."

# CHAPTER THIRTEEN

Miss Cool had not, mercifully, admitted that she was staying in the same hostelry as our mark. She had not let the excitement of the situation affect her judgement. I stuffed that fried haddock down my neck as fast as it would go, and finally began to feel right with the world. There was nothing to do in the hotel, and no sense in risking an encounter with Mr Powell, so I gently suggested a nightcap at one of the many public houses on the way back around the harbour. She declined, and instead suggested a bracing walk along to the dock end and back. It would help us both sleep, and there was at least a slim chance we might see something down at the docks.

The age difference between us was such that it was easier to see Miss Cool as a daughter than anything else, and there was never any awkwardness between us. I treated her just like any other colleague, but not as a boss like Betty always did. I saw her as a worker bee, like myself. A person of action. If her current action station happened to be mainly behind the typewriter, that didn't mean she wasn't handy in a burglary.

"Have you ever considered becoming an investigator, Miss Cool? We seem to make a habit of finding you dangerous situations on this case."

"I have. It's fun for a change, and that's true. I get the feeling you are protecting me one way or another from the more dangerous aspects of the job."

"Well, danger is usually far away. You know we get more divorces and family arguments than anything else. But it's good to know you enjoy this sort of thing when there's a need for it. Given Betty's reluctance to hire a full-time operative, or to spend any money at all, even when it's on expenses, I will try to make sure you have chances to get out on the street. You know if any harm comes to you, I'll get it in the neck anyway."

"I'll stay out of trouble then, to save your neck," she said with a smile, and strode off along the harbour wall. There was something I enjoyed about seaside towns out of season. When all the hot weather tourists had gone back to their homes, and only the real people remained. It wasn't as busy, and you could see the raw beauty of the place. The ruined Abbey up on the headland, the cliffs and the boats bobbing around. It was just like any other small town now, but one possessed of dramatic natural beauty. It was easy to see why Bram Stoker had fallen in love with the place, and easy to see why the locals had to fight off the tourists in the summer. It felt like we had the entire harbour to ourselves that evening, and it made me think more deeply about Powell's reasons for coming here. Whatever business he was handling was not official Lord Line business. It was quite clear to me that he was offloading the stuff that had been smuggled away from the main ships and concealed with the fake paperwork we had found. But why? And who for? Personal gain?

"There's one question I've been waiting to ask," Miss Cool began, tentatively, as the wind whipped her lacquered hair around her face.

"Go on," I said, leaning in to hear.

"It's about Ethel. That girl in the pub. Why are you two so close, I mean, you don't seem... on the face of it..."

"Now there's a story," I replied with a smile. As we walked, briskly in the salt air, I told her the basic outline. I didn't know what to make of her enquiry, but I enjoyed telling the story.

During our final investigation together in the police service, Betty and I had gotten involved in a case of police corruption. There was so much suspicion and finger pointing that nobody knew who to trust. There was a moment when me and Betty suspected each other. But somewhere in the middle we made a sort of pact. To see it through, no matter where it led. We never thought for a second it would lead to the office of the Lord Mayor and a complex web of his cronies, but no matter. We stuck to it. Ethel had come under unfounded suspicion as she knew some of the mayor's friends, and I hit upon the idea that she might go undercover for us. Even though she was at risk of arrest, and perhaps due to my earnestly serious expression, she agreed, and the three of us, god help us, blew the lid off the whole thing. The mayor was still languishing in the prison, fittingly close to the docks as it happens, although he was not connected to Lord Line, as far as we knew...

I became aware that I was rambling. "The truth is, Miss Cool, that Ethel's skills are not so very different from ours. She is, from my perspective, an intelligence operative. She listens and she connects and, being that she does this in places where other people drink themselves silly, she picks up far more than we can from meeting with sober people. It wouldn't work everywhere, but with one public house per street, and sometimes two, there is an underground network into which Ethel is our conduit. She should be on the books, and I take care to offload expenses to her whenever I can justify it. When you're next typing out the customer accounts, you can be sure that 'anonymous inside informant' is Ethel in nine out of ten occasions."

"So she's not, ah, romantically associated..."

I looked at Miss Cool and saw nothing of her feelings on the matter. "Not romantically, certainly not. Ethel isn't a romantic, she's a realist to the core. But you hit upon a complex area. Certainly nothing, as you would consider to be... a relationship, an affair, never. But I do have strong feelings for the girl. She's a one in a million. She has the gift. Her head is screwed on. I didn't have a sister... or a brother, of course, but... you know, I think you and Ethel have a lot in common. Different backgrounds, obviously, but similar destinations, I think..."

I suddenly had a strange thought. "Why are you asking these questions, Miss Cool, if I may speak freely?"

"I wanted to understand how much we trusted her. I was wondering... it might sound silly... but I, ah, don't have that many friends. I wondered if she might find me, or help to, you know, a boyfriend."

Well that was quite out of the range of my powers. "I see! I thought for a moment... I will see what I can do. When we're out of this particular peculiarity I will arrange it. I do see your thinking on the matter and, with certain reservations, I think Ethel might be a useful ally. It must be lonely in that office with us old timers bickering at each other."

I was in bed less than an hour later, having crept up to our rooms lest we wake Mr Powell. I never sleep well, especially not with a suspect directly above my head. There were no movements from the room when I lay down.

Three hours later, some time close to three in the morning, that changed. I was awake instantly after hearing a shuffle above. After I heard the front door open and close, I wrote Miss Cool a note and tacked it to my door in case I wasn't back in time for breakfast. I crept downstairs into the hall and across into the breakfast room. From a gap in the curtains I watched Powell in the street. He was in a hurry, and I gave chase. We followed the same walk to the harbour and long the sea wall that Miss Cool and I had carried out earlier that evening. It is always the case that understanding your surroundings is time well-spent. But something else became clear. Whatever Mr Powell was doing did not involve the formal harbour of the town. Wherever he was going, surely not far on foot, was somewhere secluded. If he was going to be picked up by a vehicle then I was finished. There would be no chance of following him at this time of night. But experience suggested he was going the whole way on foot, and he walked quickly without glancing behind.

It might have been two miles later, around half an hour, that I understood what was happening. There was a wooden jetty in an inlet ahead of us. The moonlight glinted off the water, and I heard an engine. There were two lorries parked near the jetty, and Mr Powell spoke to each of the two drivers in turn. I prostrated myself behind a dune and wished for field glasses. After another half an hour or so, during which Powell waited in the cab of a lorry, I noticed a boat hoving around the headland. Powell certainly did have his field glasses, and he jumped out of the lorry. They began to unload pallets onto the jetty using a set of wheels for moving heavy loads. I recognised such equipment as we had raced them like chariots at a warehouse I patrolled in the army. They were peculiarly low on grip on a smooth concrete floor, which gave rise to close races and full-on racing drifts. The boat approached the jetty as the last pallet came off the second truck, and the lorries retreated, never to be seen again. Powell helped the sailors load the palettes onto the boat, and off they went into the night. Powell would be walking back past my position, but I was confident that I was far enough away and out of his eyeline. He would not see me unless I sneezed or shouted.

I had no evidence for anything, not yet, but I did write down the license plates of the lorries and noted down some key features of the boat. This information would give us the chance to interrogate Powell if we wanted to, but I had to clear that with Betty first. We might choose to leave Powell in place until we unravelled more of his mysteries.

One way or another, whether this involved the Russians or not, I was certain that the contents of those palettes had been stolen from Lord Line ships. Whatever game was going on might only be personal gain, in which case Powell was Johnny on the Spot for a larger criminal enterprise.

# CHAPTER FOURTEEN

I was back at the hotel before Powell, removed the somewhat vague and coded note to Miss Cool, and managed two hours' sleep before breakfast. I was woken up by a knock on the door, groaned, and threw some clothes on. It was, mercifully, Miss Cool. I ushered her into the room and gave her the summary of my evening.

"We must not be seen together at breakfast, but I do want us both to eat breakfast there in case Powell surfaces. You go down ahead and I will follow in a few minutes, at a different table."

She nodded obediently, her eyes glowing, and I was allowed to shave in peace. As always in these places, the smell of bacon drifted into the bedrooms, summoning the occupants to feed. My expectation was that Powell would want to skip breakfast, but his only alternative would be thin Methodist gruel up at the conference hall. Nobody I knew could resist fried bacon at this hour, and I was pleased to see Miss Cool seated at the same table as Powell when I turned up. She must have been there first, and he invited himself along. I sat in the opposite corner of the room with my back to the wall and watched her work. I still hadn't seen his face, but his tall body and characteristic hairdo, as he tried in vain to conceal a bald patch, were giveaways. I watched them eat and I watched them leave, taking care to study a newspaper as Powell walked past my table. I didn't want him placing me or recognising me if he saw me again in different circs. Five minutes after Miss Cool had left, she returned.

"He's left the building," she said. "I said I would follow him up to the conference. He had some errands to run in town so I have fifteen minutes."

"No doubt sending a telegram, which is what I will be doing after we part," I said.

"He confirmed that he is a light sleeper and went out around the town for a walk. No more than that, as you would expect."

"The only way he would admit his mission last night is if it is entirely legitimate, and the fact that it happened in a concealed harbour proves otherwise. I will ask Betty what she wants us to do. I fear I will have to confront Powell very soon. Be careful, Miss Cool. Observation only today. Do not engage the quarry."

She nodded and left me to finish my meal. I caught the eye of Mrs Currie and ensured a further supply of sausages.

I used the payphone in the next street to call Betty, realising that a telegram would just waste time. She was decidedly reluctant to make a decision. "It's finely balanced," I stated. "And I think the balance rests on doing nothing. If we intercept Powell now, he will blow the whistle and we won't get the rest of the gang. I have license plates of course, and the number of the ship."

There was a pause. "You're right Ted, as usual. Give me the details and I will investigate from this end. I do wish Miss Cool was here."

"So do I."

Another pause. "Where is she, Ted?"

I realised quickly enough how to preserve the situation. "She's just gone over the road to grab a paper."

"Goodbye Ted. Call me again tonight. I'll watch for that newspaper on your expenses claim."

I planted myself on bench, half-way up the Abbey steps at lunch time. If Miss Cool came out for a walk, it would be this way, and if she remained in the garden of the conference building, I could see her. I opened up a paper and began to think of the case. It was Gelder I envied. He just upped sticks and left. I believe in his innocence, and to an extent Partridge was innocent too. But it would all rest on him. If we didn't unravel all this without more bloodshed it could be the end of his career. Men who lived mainly for work never did well if they were forced to retire. Retirement in that mansion of his with a woman he didn't trust, missing a wife he had discarded. That would be a lonely existence. Mrs Partridge herself was in a quandary. How long to wait in case Mr Gelder returned? And what was her financial position if he did not? I made a note to investigate ownership of the house but either Gelder rented it, unlikely, or he would need to sell it after things blew over. And who had offed Pearson, and why? The most obvious motive was that he had found something out, which of course meant he was innocent. Like the Salem Witches, only being murdered could prove you were totally blameless. My old shrapnel wound in my left shoulder twinged a little as I turned the page. I glanced over the top of the paper but didn't notice Miss Cool. How often mental anguish can provoke physical ailments, I noted, and continued to read. Waiting on a stakeout was the worst part of this job. Midnight action appealed to me, it kept me a little younger and kept things interesting. But sitting on a bench with the temperatures hovering around zero and a wind blowing in off the sea was not my idea of fun.

Finally, something happened. If Miss Cool did notice me and came out to talk, she would need to make sure that Powell wasn't watching from inside the building. Had she thought of that? Yes she had, she was approaching the fence, looking aimless, with a note in her hand. She casually stuffed it into the chain-link and sauntered off. She appeared to be calm and without haste. I would take her note to read, returning at four o'clock to follow her if she emerged with Powell.

The note indicated that our trip was coming to an end. Powell had told her during the morning tea break that he was going home tomorrow. That suggested, she said, and I agreed, another shipment tonight and then home on the first train. I decided there and then that we would be on the same train. All we had to do was record the particulars of all the vehicles involved, and I decided also that Miss Cool should be present. She would learn from the experience and her younger eyes might even prove useful.

All went to plan. Miss Cool dined once again with Powell, and he even went as far as giving her a hug outside the hotel. Thank God he didn't choose to do it inside under the watch of Mrs Currie. Everyone went to bed nice and early, and I rose at midnight to collect Miss Cool and put ourselves in position at the coast before Powell set off.

We arrived at the headland and found my vantage point to lie down in. It gave a good view of the approach Powell would make on foot, the parking place for the lorries, and the jetty itself. Of course, I had deliberately forgotten to check in with Betty.

Half an hour later, things started to happen.

"Here's the first lorry," I said. "Powell should go and sit in the cab. There were two lorries yesterday and then sometime later the boat will show up."

"There he is!" whispered Miss Cool. She watched silently as Powell climbed aboard the cab. Shortly after, a second lorry arrived. Miss Cool noted the licence plates and we both cast our eyes out to sea.

Half an hour later, the boat's light appeared in the distance. Powell had the advantage of binoculars and would have seen the boat before us.

"Hang on a minute," said Miss Cool. "Don't you recognise that driver sitting next to Mr Powell?"

I looked, screwing up my eyes. I did not. And, more to the point, how did Miss Cool know him?

"He's the security guard from that night when we burgled the filing cabinet!"

"I knew there was a reason to bring you," I said, elated. License plates were important but a direct connection from these goings on to the Lord Line was vital. "Thank you, that's extremely helpful. We'd better get back. As soon as Powell leaves, we will follow him. The first train is at seven o'clock tomorrow morning so we won't get much sleep."

# CHAPTER FIFTEEN

Miss Cool stood alone on the platform, with me at the other end, almost out of sight in the mist. As we had hoped, Mr Powell saw her straight away and they sat together all the way home.

As soon as we arrived at the railway station, Miss Cool said goodbye to Powell, looped back around and met me back inside the station. We walked in silence back to the office, ready to fully brief Betty on our unexpectedly fruitful seaside Methodist retreat. The only thing we had to edit was to make it look like all the dangerous stuff had happened to me. We were certain that Powell had ordered the disappearance of Pearson. We just didn't know who had carried out the deed.

Afterwards, and at a loose end, I felt obliged to visit Mrs Partridge at that quiet, dark, Gelder house in Anlaby. Whenever there was a conspiracy, a group within a group, a traitor, a betrayal, it was the innocent who suffered the most. The guilty, like Powell, always expect to be caught and plan to avoid it. They're prepared for the worst. The innocent feel aggrieved, injured, and they start to suspect each other. Perhaps Partridge and Gelder had first fallen out over the smuggling. Maybe each suspected the other. Stress at work boiled over at home, and Mrs Partridge switched camps, finally breaking the friendship between her two partners. And now, with people being murdered, Gelder had thrown in the towel. Perhaps he wasn't as innocent as he claimed, even if it had just been deliberately not seeing something. And now Mrs Partridge was left again to pick up the pieces and plan for an uncertain future.

"The most natural thing would be to return to Mr Partridge," she said as she handed me a cup of tea. "Do you think that woman will lose interest?"

"No I don't," I admitted. "Not if she's really in it for the money. But there is something more going on. That's why I came." I lied, of course. Always more polite.

"Some valuers came. Said they were on behalf of the family. Once the legal time period is up they will declare Alfred dead and sell the house, so they might as well get prepared. I told them to sling their hooks."

"Quite right, Mrs Partridge. Mr Gelder is only missing, officially. What are your theories about the new lady of the manor?"

"Isn't it simple, Mr Bird? It's always the simple answer. Money. She's fun on a night out, and by her own yardstick she's decent enough. But she lacks one thing and that's money."

"She lacks a family. Don't all women want that? That's what the men are told."

"We never wanted children. Well, perhaps I did, at first. But I wasn't born into money and it ruins people. It really does corrupt them. Partridge didn't have any money and he worshipped it, truth be told. And once you make some, you spend some, and you need more. I'm only as religious as manners dictate, Mr Bird, but money is an evil thing for its own sake."

"You don't think he's involved in the smuggling?"

"No. I'm certain of that. But there is something you should know. When I look back over the last year, I have a conviction that things started to go wrong at work around the same time that woman arrived in our lives. Why should that be?"

"The mind plays tricks, Mrs Partridge. It's natural to collect all your misfortune together like that. The mind is wonderful, and deceitful, in equal measure."

"Have a look at the dates, then. Just to rule it out. I began to suspect Mr Partridge in March and by April I was out on my ear, and she was moving into the big house. Mr Gelder was appalled, and one thing led to another."

"Mrs Partridge, leave it with me."

I wish I had time to check Mrs Partridge's theories out but Powell was now the sole focus of our enquiries. We had him linked to the Lord Line, thanks to Miss Cool's sharp eyes, via one of the security men. Betty had linked all of the trucks to the company, which likely meant the drivers were being bribed to make the additional journeys. We knew, as we had all along, that this was a large gang and that one day, one of them would slip up. Powell must be near the top of the leadership of the ring, if not the top. He hid behind a mask of respectability with his active Methodist learnings and teachings. He even had a secretary or filing clerk involved in faking up the paper trail. Perhaps that was a useful line of enquiry. But had he killed Pearson? It seemed more likely that he arranged for Pearson to have an accident. Men like that, the lynchpins, don't do anything criminal themselves. Nothing they could swing for. And why had he started this elaborate enterprise last spring, if that was when it all started? And if Mrs Partridge was even half right, a thought to make you shudder, then Lana Turner was somehow involved as well. I set up a meeting with Partridge at the office to see if he was getting anywhere on the inside.

"I can't think of a good way to ask, Mr Partridge, except to ask how well you know Miss Turner?"

It was clearly the right question, because he leapt out of his seat and stood with his back to me, looking out to the river and to sea. "I've been asking myself that, and the simple answer is, not very well."

"Is there any possibility..."

"I really don't know. I don't. I don't know her at all. At least with Mrs..."

I decided to wait. It was always better to wait, however long it took. I crossed my legs and sipped my tea. I looked out over Mr Partridge's shoulder to the murky river and wondered how many countries it led to. There was nothing more fascinating than ships. Trains could only take you over the land to places in the same country. A ship could take you anywhere on earth, if you had the patience. One day, ships would rule the world. Once people realised that ships could take anything, anywhere, the world would become a smaller place. Perhaps they would take cargo more interesting than steel and wood. On the other hand, perhaps there *was* nothing more exciting than steel and wood. From such raw materials you could make anything you wanted, and things that you didn't know you wanted.

"I couldn't put Lana on that list," he said. "I just couldn't. You wouldn't have believed it. You would have sought her out first. You wouldn't have taken me seriously *at all*. How can you trust a man who has no idea who he lives with?"

"I'm not sure any of us know that, except those of us who live alone," I replied. "I agree that putting her name on the list would have changed my approach. Although, if you remember, she pretty much was the first person I visited, but for a different reason. I wrongly assumed you had been married for years and she would help me understand if you were playing a straight bat."

Partridge turned, with full eyes. "Yes, it's true. You did seek her out. You wouldn't be the first. Men just *like* Lana. I was the one with the money, I suppose, which is why she chose me."

"You don't think there's any chance she is involved in... whatever is going on?"

"Of course there is! The timelines, what you people would call the timelines, match up. Things turned sour almost the moment she arrived."

It seems that the Partridges still thought alike. "But she can't be directly involved, surely. I mean, she doesn't work here. She's not actively smuggling stuff."

"She certainly has the capability to control any man on my staff, if she chose to. Those cocktail evenings. She has access to many of the senior managers at Lord Line."

It was clear Lana Turner had the access she would need, but I couldn't even begin to think what her motive was. If it was money, then Partridge had enough to fulfil any ambition she could have. He was the richest man in the county. If it wasn't money, then I was at square one.

"It's not money," he explained, unnecessarily. "Whatever she's doing isn't about money."

"I think it's time to start thinking about where she came from, her past. We need to understand Miss Turner rather better than we do today."

Partridge nodded. "You have my permission. Speak to anyone you need to. I have to know."

The only obvious next step was to interview Ethel about her friend from years ago. What did she know, what did she suspect? What *didn't* she know?

"We all have our suspicions about everyone we ever met, Ted," replied Ethel, enigmatically.

"She just disappeared, overnight, without a word? It's not such a big town, and with your connections-"

She rested a hand on my arm. "You're too logical, Ted. It's not that big of a town, but there are hundreds of girls like me and Lana. It was a few weeks before I noticed I hadn't seen her, and she wasn't at the address I had for her and none of us were on the phone back then. This was twenty years ago. She did disappear, but not in a way that made me think she was in danger. There were no headlines, no rumours. She just stopped being mentioned."

"And your number one suspicion, if you had to take a wild stab in the dark on a foggy night?"

"The most logical answer, of which you would approve, but to my mind doesn't quite capture the full story, would be that she had a child and went away to give birth to her baby."

"And afterwards, she had to either give the baby away or totally change her approach to life. Either one equally possible, do you think?" I tried to lead her, to cause a reaction.

"If you think Lana would ever have given anything up, much less her own flesh and blood, then you don't know her. And of course, *you* don't know her. I do. I promise you that if that girl ever got pregnant, she would love that child and keep him close to the end of her days."

Ethel spoke with such passion, such finality, that I wasted no time. If Lana had a baby, who would now be around twenty years of age, I would find him.

# CHAPTER SIXTEEN

If Lana Turner had a child who was now a man, around the age of twenty, who could he be? Someone like Southman would fit the bill. He was the right age, and the assumption was that he would work his way upwards. But he had been at the company for years, much longer than Miss Turner's tenure in this scene. If he was her son, then it was *him* helping *her*, not the other way around. I would think he didn't much like her interfering in his job prospects, and mainly for the worse. And what was all that about the Russians? If he was involved with her than all the Russian stuff was false.

There was only one thing for it. Cocoa and bed. I picked up the fake bills of lading to read again. It was one of those nights when several new leads multiplied the possibilities. A case that you expected to go in one direction now had several forks in the road. You had to test out each new piece separately against what you knew or suspected, and then try more than one piece at a time. There was only one solution, and it involved every piece fitting neatly. This was the only kind of jigsaw I enjoyed. One with a purpose.

As I stared at the paperwork, front and back, upside down and inside out, I became convinced that Miss Turner was a fraud and that Southman was straight up, just like Partridge. I decided to test what I knew with these fixed facts. They were not really fixed, but I had years of experience and intuition to work on. Partridge and Southman, Gelder and Pearson were all playing straight. Powell was corrupt. Lana Turner was hiding something and probably involved. I pulled out the original list Partridge had given me at the start. It was crumpled and stained now, torn and harder to read. But of course, there had been five names on that list. The name of Charles Wilson stared back out at me. He was a little over twenty. He was the right age to be the son of Lana Turner, and although he hadn't struck me as treacherous or lying, I couldn't rule it out. He would have to be approached once again, and my instinct told me that Miss Cool would be the one to do it. She had proven herself with Powell and I felt she would get to the truth faster than I could. One way or another, the net was closing, and Miss Turner could throw the whole case if she found out we were talking to Wilson. I hatched the plan. I would approach Wilson tomorrow with Miss Cool, and for insurance I would have Betty with Miss Turner at the house, in case any messages came in. We had one clear chance to strike without any of them being on their guard. After tomorrow, the panic might start to set in, and things always happened fast if people panicked.

Panic never ended in a predictable way, and with Pearson dead already I decided to speak to the police before I did anything at all. With this set in my mind, sleep came quicker than I hoped.

My first meeting was with Inspector Givens, and I laid out the bare bones of what we knew, and what I suspected, including the trip to Whitby and the connections we had made since. Even his most enigmatic expression suggested he was impressed at how much I had uncovered in such a short space of time. "Of course," he said, "an inter-jurisdictional investigation of this kind would have taken weeks to organise officially. You can just travel wherever your fancy takes you."

That was as close as he would get to a compliment. My next visit was to Betty to make sure she had just enough information to agree to stake out the Partridge house and, if possible, gain entry to watch Miss Turner at close quarters. Once she was out of the way I summoned Miss Cool into my office for a thorough briefing. I laid on the danger quite thickly, to make sure she realised that this was a different prospect to Powell. If I was right, if Mr Wilson was the son of Lana Turner, if he was the carry-outer of whatever strategies Powell had thought up, it most likely meant he was the killer of Pearson and he would be more likely to kill again if he was placed under too much pressure. Miss Cool seemed to understand this logic, and to her credit she did not shrink from the task.

"The key is to get him to talk quickly, without spooking him into calling mummy," was as brief as I could be. "We must leave everything still in play, with nobody panicking or shutting things down. We want everything in play so that we can watch from a distance. If you need to mention that stupid memoir cover story, do so. Don't mention Powell or Whitby, not unless Wilson mentions it first. And don't mention Lana Turner unless he does so first. Start with Gelder, whom I know to be innocuous, and then move to Powell if the moment seems right. Let him do the talking. And come out either as soon as you can link him to Powell, or if you sense danger. Figure out a signal you can use to alert me. If you use the signal, I will come in all guns blazing and get you out of there, but that must be a last resort. The signal means danger."

She nodded quietly. "I understand, Mr Bird. This is a real assignment, isn't it?"

"Oh yes, Miss Cool. This is the man. And if he's not we need to know anyway."

"If I sense danger I will take out my makeup mirror and start to touch my face. If you see that mirror come out, I've blown it."

"I wouldn't say it like that. This is a delicate operation. Anyone could blow it. But with your observation and intuition I think you have a better chance with Wilson than I do. If I go back to him for a second visit he will immediately be on guard. With you, we have a chance that he will let enough slip that we'll be able to link him to Turner and Powell."

And that was the setup. In a sense it was out of my hands. My job was to not let Miss Cool out of my sight and scoop her out of there if it went south.

# CHAPTER SEVENTEEN

It all seemed too neat somehow, and there were still some problems with the theory. I was convinced that Wilson was Lana Turner's son, making her real name Miss Wilson. She had never been married and had seen the arrival of her son as a misfortune, but somehow had stayed out of the poorhouse or any other institution and made sure he received adequate education. But sometime after that, times had turned for her, and she had looked him up. One way or another they had hatched a plan to worm her way into Mr Partridge's orbit at a time when it was common knowledge that he had problems at home. Presumably, if Partridge had not been an open goal, she would have worked her way down the list to Gelder and the others. But persistence paid off, and eventually she installed herself in the Partridge home as the supposed next Mrs Partridge.

This hung together, to a point. Perhaps that same ambition was what drove young Wilson to smuggling and corruption. If Powell was the mastermind, Wilson was merely one of his foot soldiers. He needed quite a few, and Wilson had an ace up his sleeve, if he needed it: his mummy was sleeping with the big boss, which meant they had an early warning system if he became suspicious. He had indeed become suspicious, which is why he hired me, and we could assume Lana Turner had been feeding information to Wilson and Powell since the first moment. It was lucky I had deployed Miss Cool on Powell, for sure, because if I had been seen in Whitby, Powell would have been expecting me. This all seemed quite logical and the problem with logic is that life isn't at all logical. Tempting though it was to think that this explained everything, it didn't come close.

Although I didn't like being someone else's puppet, I was gratified that at least Partridge had been straight up with us. I didn't mind being messed around by the great beauty of Miss Turner. No man would. That's the problem with great beauty. You forgive it anything, even murder. That's why she was so important to this gang. Wilson would only have embarked on this route if he though his legitimate career had either stalled or was stunted. His impatience had gotten the better of him. Perhaps his mother had forced him to help her using whatever leverage she chose. More likely, Powell had helped fix up Lana Turner with Partridge. He would have introduced them, at the suggestion of young Wilson, and he would have seen the advantages immediately. He was a ruthless criminal who had killed Pearson when he began to get wind of the smuggling racket.

I decided to run this past Betty because there was something not sitting right. Very little of Southman's theories were necessary to make this smuggling and corruption fit the known information, which might mean he was simply a plant to throw us off the scent. Or every word he said was true and we had somehow missed a much bigger picture.

That was when Miss Cool returned, so Betty and I debriefed her as we rolled Jimmy Southman's yarns around our mouths.

"I guarantee that Lana is Charlie Wilson's mother, making her Lana Wilson," said Miss Cool as she flung her coat at the hat stand. "No doubt at all."

I watched with admiration as her confidence grew every time I put her in danger. Miss Cool was old enough to make her own decisions in the eyes of the law, but Betty would blame any mishap on me and we both knew her prime concern would be the loss of a very competent receptionist and one of the fastest and most accurate dictators in the city, a claim which I found highly amusing.

"Look," said Betty, "it's simple. Our client doesn't know about the Russian mumbo jumbo coming out of Southman's addled brain. It's not our problem. The whole story holds tight together, and it goes like this. Powell is the ringmaster and he's on the take in a big way. He has influence enough to fix the accounts to hide the crime, and influence enough to bribe a few security guards and drivers and he's got better at it the longer he's gone uncaught. Wilson is one of his little worker bees, and it's a bonus, or deliberate, that his mother has wheedled her way into Partridge's affections. This means that she's been spying on us, and more specifically, Ted, you, since the beginning. But Partridge doesn't trust her and gave her all that yack about the book too. Sometime later, they realised you were a detective and after more than a good story, and that's when Pearson died. He died to frame you and it nearly worked. Gelder got spooked, so that he and Partridge are honest and on the level. Powell, Wilson the son and Wilson the mother are all involved. Partridge might try to keep the Wilsons out of it because then he can keep his firm's reputation intact. Southman is either jealous, a fantasist, or is part of a different conspiracy. But my suggestion, in fact, my formal request as your employer, is that you both keep schtum about Southman until we've been paid and the case is officially closed."

I couldn't trust any of them. Apart from Betty and Miss Cool, every single other person was subject to a greater or lesser degree of suspicion. You could get to a point where you almost trusted someone, and it's always a bonus when you can trust your client, but as the pressure builds, there is always a chance that someone trusted will do a stupid thing. That's why speed and momentum are so crucial. The longer a case drags on, the greater the chance that a perfectly honest, logical citizen could go crazy and ruin everything. The one person who could shed light on Southman's Russia ravings was most likely Inspector Givens. And he would also need to provide support, not to say legitimacy, to any final showdown, should one become necessary.

"Everything you told me last time checks out," said Givens as we sat together in my office with Betty. "Miss Turner has never been married and she did have a son, and her real name is Wilson. I know what school she went to. We, or at least, my former colleagues, picked her up a few times in her later teen years through to her early twenties but then she seems to have straightened out when she had a baby. She worked as a housekeeper here and there, building a reputation and keeping her nose clean until Wilson himself hit his teens. She gave birth young. She's still not thirty-five, if you can believe it, but something changed recently. For whatever reason, she needed help from her son. Maybe she had acquired a debt of some kind, an enemy, I don't know yet. But she needed help and he figured that cutting her in on his black-market activities would be helpful, and he persuaded Powell to cut her in. That's all conjecture, but Powell has previous. We did some digging around in his previous life, down near Birmingham, and he has a rap sheet as long as your arm. He must have done some fast work to get the references he needed to work at a respectable place like Lord Line and once he got in, he worked hard and kept out of trouble. People revert to type when they hit some kind of pressure. Maybe boredom, maybe realising that he would never get into Gelder's orbit of the inner circle meant he would never win overall control of the company when Partridge eventually retires. Whatever happened, he started to use the company to further his own ends, smuggling cargo here and there to boost his salary, and building a tight network within the company to help him. That's where the friendly security guards and truck drivers come into it. Some of them no doubt just work cash in hand and don't really know what they're involved in. All of this checks out."

"Have you come across any Russians?" I asked him, relieved as much as anything that he, a trusted former colleague, was seeing things as I saw them.

"None at all. But your Mr Southman is not as straight as you might think, he does have a past of his own to boast about. But there are several years we can't account for. I think we need to put some pressure on him pretty quickly to get some big answers out of him. I don't understand where his Russians come into the picture. Quite honestly, were it not for him, this whole case would rather look solved to me."

He was right. If you neglected Southman's allegations, it was a simple case of an honest businessman, Partridge, alighting on some corruption which, having failed to understand, he sought the outside help of a private investigator, who eventually joined some dots that were too painful for Mr Partridge to join on his own. That investigation, once it became common knowledge, led to the murder of Pearson, who at once seemed innocent, having paid the ultimate price, and Gelder, who was also innocent but afraid of following Pearson into the murky waters with concrete boots. He legged it before things got too heavy. It all fitted like the perfect jigsaw. The amazing thing was that *nothing* Southman had said about Russians made any sense. "So," I said eventually, "Southman is also a rogue but working to a different agenda. He might be throwing lies around to conceal Powell's activities. Or he might be acting for another master, but he seemed straight enough to me. My radar didn't sniff out anything. He seemed to be helping me, if anything."

"Okay. We need to know. The Chief wants this closing up before anyone else bites the dust. We'll come up with a plan now and it needs putting into action tonight. Tomorrow morning is when people start getting arrested, and we sure as hell need to make sure we arrest the right people."

# CHAPTER EIGHTEEN

It all happened down at the docks that night. I told you that at the beginning, didn't I? Now you're in a position to understand the stakes, you're on the same page as me.

If you know this town, you know that there are a *lot* of docks. Even within a single quay there are so many docks and berths that you can't see a single one. They merge together like ships on the horizon. Nothing I can say to you will help you to understand that 'the docks' area is larger than most towns, and just as busy. We had to know *which* part of *which* dock, and we cut it fine.

Partridge only used the King's Dock, which cut it down, but it's the largest. The King's Dock unloads some of the biggest ships ever built, from all around the world. All kinds of produce and machinery, food, even live animals. It takes the lot. Being the town's biggest shipping line meant we didn't even know which of his boats was going to stage the action.

If the Titanic hadn't sank, it might have been at the King's Dock last night. But for one important fact. The only thing the King's Dock does not carry is people. No human passengers. Strictly freight.

Betty was all for taking guns to the show. I've always refused to carry and I didn't see any reason to change my mind, but I believed she and Partridge both took pistols. I doubted hers would stop a bird, but it made her relax a notch.

It was just as foggy last night as that first morning I met Partridge. It should have been a sign. I never trusted him, but then I never trust any of our clients. Betty has her eyes only on the money, and that's fine. But I have my eyes on my own backside, as the law won't protect me if I break it, no matter how much I want to blame her. Criminality is the responsibility of the individual. I had seen nothing to convince me that Partridge was playing it fully straight with us, and events supported me. Such men, and I understand their point of view, tell you what you need to know. In coming to us, to Betty, he was showing a certain weakness, an exasperation on a matter he viewed as delicate. It was an admission of failure that led him to us. He had ample supply of men to do his bidding, so I never bought that he was desperate. He could have handled the matter with his own resources, if he chose to. It goes to figure that he was somehow manipulating us. He had an agenda in paying us for stuff he could have done cheaper on his own. The only surprise was that the mole lived under his own roof. Sometimes you just need to have a suspicion to put you on your guard, and I managed to get out of it last night with mine and Betty's reputations in the clear.

So where do you want me to start? I told Betty to go to bed, of course, but she wouldn't hear of it. Eleven of the clock found me stood next to Betty, waist deep in fog, drizzle falling parallel to the ground and the wind gusting it upwards as much as down. We were out by the old warehouses, some distance off from the action. The ship wasn't due for a couple of hours.

Half an hour after we showed up, a long car pulled into the car parking area. Partridge got out, spoke to his chauffeur, and the car vanished as silently as it arrived. Partridge marched into the offices where it's warm. We didn't see him for another hour. But the feeling is of *people*. I felt like there were large numbers of men dotted around the docks in anticipation. They were not normally there, hence the anticipation, and they were likely on a bonus. It seemed too quiet to me. They were unseen and trying hard not to breathe, which as you know will always make you pant like an old dog after an uphill run in the sun.

"Christ you should have brought a gun, you idiot," said Betty. "You're the only sucker without one tonight."

It was something to say. I blew some smoke in her direction, but the wind took it into my eyes. I blinked. The only certainty, apart from the weather and the shooters, was that Lana Turner was not here tonight. Betty was the only woman. Whatever she had done, whatever her reasons, she was absent.

We waited some more. The rain got worse. If anything, the night got darker as the slit of moon went behind a cloud. I turned up my collar. Betty tutted. No collar for her. But she had hot metal for company. We waited.

I walked up and I walked down. Betty worked across ways, stomping out a crucifix that nobody would ever see. I thought she was altering her pace to make sure we bumped each other. We stopped again, huddling together in a way that made me feel uncomfortable. Where was everyone? Where was the ship? Was it late in the fog?

At last, I heard the ship horns. There were two things to note. As far as the ship's crew were concerned there was nothing to hide, this was a routine unlading. They would be loaded up and gone again ready for the next tide. The river in this part of town has always been tidal. It's an estuary, remember, which makes it great for properly big ships but not so great if you get held up by a tide. When the river sucks out into the sea, we're left with a lot of mud instead.

The other thing, which follows on from this being a routine trip, is that the ship must use its horn. The funny thing is that you get so used to those rumbling horns that you stop hearing them. I doubt there was anyone on that dock there at that moment that didn't hear it. I heard a noise that wasn't a cheer, but it was definitely the sound of relief. Perhaps someone had finally been forced to breath out. I heard footsteps in the distance.

"Christ alive," said Betty. "Eyes down." She blew smoke and drove the butt into the stony ground. That was when she unfurled the field glasses, one pair. I screwed my eyes up and reckoned I could see enough. The ship was coming alongside. Shouting. Ropes being thrown and knotted.

We didn't know what Partridge was about, but we wouldn't be waiting long to find out. Would he have some police there to try and arrest anyone he suspected? Everything I knew about Partridge made me think that he was going to handle this himself, that we were here, paid by him, as witnesses, and whatever we were going to see was a form of enactment. We were likely to be the most independent eyes on that dock, and we were being paid by him.

"There's money here, somewhere," said Betty, in a strange panting voice. She jolted the glasses up and along the boat, then to the offices where Partridge had been waiting, then back to the boat. Calculations were being made in that head of hers.

And suddenly we were off. There was Partridge, storming out of the main office building with a handful of cronies. They had really set their caps into the wind and rain and were haring off towards the ship. A few seconds later, delayed by the action of running to their cars and getting them started, a car sped in from each side of the scene, aimed towards the ship. It was an ambitious pincer movement intended to leave no prisoners.

My instinct was to join the fray, and I knew Betty was making the same internal debate as me. Was there something we hadn't thought of, some unseen hand or actor ready to pounce? Should we rush in?

"We can't see anything from here," I said at last, and set off towards the action with Betty trotting a couple of paces behind. I thought she was waving that gun of hers, but more likely she was holding it inside her coat ready for action. There wasn't time to check.

We had no cover, and in that we were no worse off than anyone else. It felt like half the town was here, marching across this dock. It wasn't anywhere near as desolate as it had been. People were running this way and that, only they themselves knowing what role was theirs. Were they unloading the ship? Were they with Partridge? Or against him? Who was allied to whom?

Something dramatic and abrupt happened then, as we all arrived at the ship. The first gun was yanked out into the open. This inevitably drew out several others. I was right. Betty had been concealing her firearm and continued to do so. There were so many guns that one would get fired, and a domino would begin. This is exactly why—

There was a bang. The sound is always higher pitched than you expect, especially with the metal hulk of the ship to ricochet off. Was it something being dropped on board? There was no obvious reprisal to the shot, if it had been a shot, confounding my experience.

"Stop there!" shouted old man Partridge. Evidently he had sieved this crazy scene and located his enemy, the man who had been siphoning off substantial fractions of his ships for several months now. Partridge was too wise to hold a weapon himself, but the men either side of him had their pistols trained on the same figure. It was a small man wearing a trilby, his shoes shinier than anyone else's out there, shinier somehow in the rain. The buckles magnified the small amount of light there was.

I recognised that figure. It wasn't a man, it was Lana Turner herself! Had Partridge noticed this? She had been unable to resist this major event, unable to remain prone on the chaise, sipping a cocktail with that male friend of hers that turned out to be her son. She was still playing this game, after everything they had been through. She was intent on pulling a weapon out of her pocket, even with two or three trained back at her. What on earth was she doing?

"Drop it!" shouted Partridge. "Drop it you idiot!"

"You won't have them shoot me, you buffoon!" She started laughing then, and slowly placed the gun on the ground in front of her. She flicked her boot at the weapon and it sailed across the ground towards Partridge. "Lana?" he said at last. The old fool bent to pick the gun up. What was he thinking?

"Why did he do that?" asked Betty, possibly of herself.

"I think it's the shock of it," I said. Look. The wind's gone out of him.

"Lana? You're behind all this?"

"Stand these goons down and let's talk inside. It'll take a while, but I can explain it, honestly Donald."

"This weapon is warm," he stated. "What happened on board?"

The certainty seemed to dim in her eyes then. We had the weapon, but who did it belong to? I felt a sudden rush of certainty that Lana wasn't going to be shooting anyone. "I can explain it all quietly, not out here in the rain."

Thank god things seemed to be quietening down without anyone else being hurt. The goons were getting edgy, shifting their weight between feet. One of them looked at Partridge, then back to Lana.

"That sounds like the best idea I've heard all night," Betty said at last. "Let's quit the standoff out here and get some hot chocolate."

The sheer incongruity of her contribution dissolved the tension, and we solemnly made our way back to the office, Betty and I walking behind Partridge and Miss Turner, or Wilson as we now knew her to be. The goons sharply disappeared into the cars and rumbled away into the shadows.

I wasn't sure how Partridge was going to take these revelations. His reaction would be controlled by the expectations of his generation. She had embarrassed him, led him on a wild goose chase, and someone had fired a gun at god knew whom. This would take a lot of sorting out.

But that was the last thought I had that evening because there was another surprise gunshot from close quarters, and when I looked down I found my own blood running down towards my ankle. My head snapped around to see Betty's shock. The blood was draining from her face. "Oh Ted!" she said. "It just slipped!" And they tell me I fainted dead away.

I couldn't sleep in the infirmary. Nobody can, not on the first night. If I had my druthers it would be my last. The bullet had gone straight through without touching bone or vital organs, a graze. I was in the clear. Just a precaution. But the look on Betty's face was compensation enough. I could sense a cash bonus coming. Danger money.

You will want to know who fired the pistol and why it wasn't thrown overboard to hide the evidence. Through luck and idiocy so many people touched that gun that the police won't be able to charge anyone, but the most important fact is that me and Betty solved the case, helped immensely by Miss Cool, and we collected the money from Partridge in full with a bonus for tactful judgement. He didn't want Miss Wilson's involvement in the whole thing to get any wind in its sails, but I expected

Mrs Partridge to return within the week and for Charlie Wilson and his mother to leave town in Gelder's wake.

Notwithstanding what lies the cuckoos were all chirping at the police as I reclined in a hard bed with a thin mattress, this is what I think happened. It was Mr Powell who was shot, of course, and they found him dead on the ship. I wouldn't swear to it, but I believe there was a scuffle instigated by Charlie Wilson. Powell is the one, we presume, who asked Charlie to get rid of Pearson, and with Powell gone, Charlie could just as easily pin Pearson on Powell and neaten up all the ends. If he had thrown the gun that might have been the end of it, but luckily for him, his mother had noticed it and decided to handle it herself, and then coincidentally mishandle it such that Partridge felt obliged to pick it up. With so many prints on it they could invent any story they thought would serve their interests.

And there you have it. Only one of the guns last night truly slipped and it was Betty's, or at least, I sincerely hope it slipped. The Wilson gun that put the fatal bullet into Powell was only made to look as if it slipped, to cover the guilt of Charlie. That was the end of our case, and a successful one that would be all over the papers tomorrow. We would have wall to wall divorces beating a path to our door. But as I drifted off to sleep again, thanks to the painkillers, it was Southman who occupied my thoughts. His ravings about the Russians had seemed careful, not ravings at all, and it cast a light shadow over our success.

*Ted Bird and Betty Abbett will return...*

Look out for **BAD HEIST** by Ernest McQueen later in 2021. The long-awaited second book featuring Ted Bird and Betty Abbett from Mad Dog Crime is available for pre-order right now at

**www.maddogbooks.uk**

You can also sign up for our free email newsletter. Subscribers get free gifts, discounts and first news of our latest titles.

## Credits

Mad Dog Crime would like to thank all those who volunteered to read and review this book before publication, especially the friends and family of the author. In addition, particular thanks are given to a small number of readers who pre-ordered this story, sight unseen, in far corners of the world. Special thanks go to Dave Werran and Mark Webster. We hope you enjoy this book.

## Other Books by WTD Books / Mad Dog Crime

*by Paul Charles*
From Beyond Belief / The Playground
Kicking Tin

*by P. C. DETTMANN*
Paul Locksley
Nikoo Hayek
Ernest Zevon
Jorja Pearson

*by Ernest McQueen*
The Gun Slipped
Bad Heist